CRITICAL PRAISE FOR ALEX WHEATLE

- Finalist for the 2021 NSK Neustadt Prize
  for Children's Literature
- Winner of the *Guardian* Children's Fiction Prize 2016
- Nominated for the CILIP Carnegie Medal 2017
- Short-listed for the YA Book Prize 2018

For *Cane Warriors*

"The importance of this book cannot be overstated. Alex Wheatle takes the truth and creates fiction to illuminate that truth. He too is a warrior—a word warrior. I saw my ancestors in this book, and now I know that Alex and I really are brothers."
　　　　　　　　　—Benjamin Zephaniah, author of *Gangsta Rap*

"Alex Wheatle is a master storyteller. He writes with urgency, passion, and the empathy we all need to wrestle with the realities of transatlantic slavery, bringing marginalized narratives straight out of the shadows, right into the frame. Every kid in the country needs to read this book."　　　—Jeffrey Boakye, author of *Black, Listed*

For *Home Girl*

"With a tough exterior and brash attitude, Naomi is an authentic character in an unfortunate yet accurate picture of modern-day foster care in the UK . . . The ending is neither predictable nor sugarcoated, leaving readers rooting for this determined heroine."
　　　　　　　　　　　　　　　　—*School Library Journal*

"Wheatle returns to the world of his award-winning Crongton books with his most powerful and personal novel yet. Naomi Brisset is a teenage girl growing up too fast in the UK care system. Her journey through a series of foster homes exposes the unsettling, often heart-wrenching truth of this life. Yet despite the grit, Wheatle's writing is as rich and warm as ever, bringing courage and hope to an unforgettable heroine's story."
　　　　　　　　　　　　　—*Bookseller* (UK), Editor's Choice

"Teenager Naomi, old before her time and as vulnerable as she is fierce, is growing up in the care system. Foster homes and pupil referral units revealing the unsettling, often bewildering reality of this existence. Wheatle's empathy, authentic characters, and rich dialogue illuminate the dark." —*Observer Magazine* (UK)

"Another powerful and poignant novel deftly created by one of the most prolific master novelists on either side of the pond. *Home Girl* is a page-turner, with not a dull moment. Loved it from the rooter to the tooter." —Eric Jerome Dickey, *New York Times* best-selling author of *Before We Were Wicked*

"Alex Wheatle's latest novel offers no unrealistic fairy tale happy ending. But the award-winning writer, who draws on his own experiences of a childhood in care, does offer some hope for Naomi, a sometimes difficult but very likable heroine." —*Irish News*, Children's Book of the Week

"Wheatle has delivered a definitive narrative steeped in cultural philosophy and human sensibilities. Despite the foibles of his tragic characters, a redemptive quality is present—persevering—a testament of the human will to survive against all odds . . . Highly recommended." —*Kaieteur News* (Guyana)

For *Home Boys*

"Wheatle writes in an unadorned and realistic style with a keen ear for the natural language of children and young adults. Doubtless, readers will experience a sense of triumph at the strength and solidarity of the survivors and a burning desire to see the many real-life abusers and those who covered up for them brought to justice." —*Morning Star* (UK)

"This book is impossible to put down. A tale of camaraderie, survival, and revenge, *Home Boys* is in parts a British equivalent of Stephen King's classic *Stand By Me*, albeit with a more immediate and harrowing background." —*Buzz Magazine* (UK)

"It's hard to imagine a gritty-realism novel about emotional, physical, and sexual abuse in children's homes also being a beautifully written poetic portrayal of loyalty, friendship, and boyhood adventure. Wheatle, however, manages to blend the two into one perfectly painted story. The underlying themes of friends replacing family, childhood shaping adulthood, and the very thin line that separates madness and sanity combine to produce a horrifying account of under-privilege."   —*Big Issue* (UK)

"Alex Wheatle's book confirms his status as the UK's leading contemporary novelist chronicling black urban life. Wheatle has written about a highly controversial subject matter with sensitivity and maturity, marking him out of future greatness as a writer who is prepared to face the darker sides of humankind and in the process forcing us to ask questions of our society and of ourselves as individuals."   —*The Badger* (UK)

For *The Seven Sisters*

"A gripping, horrifying, and moving adventure story about children brought up without parents, trying to survive on the run."
        —Maggie Gee, author of *Virginia Woolf in Manhattan*

"Wheatle's picture of childhood in a care home evokes the trauma and the tenderness between four friends, as well as brilliantly recreating a lost era. *The Seven Sisters* is subtle, moving, and written with real moral and artistic purpose."   —Ben Richards

"With a friendship of unspoken confidences remaining the focus, the four boys negotiate a mutual search for understanding and freedom. The narrative is strong and meaningful."
                           —*Independent on Sunday* (UK)

"This is a brave, brutal story told with a shocking immediacy. Alex Wheatle has created a disturbing portrait of life in a children's home, in language which is plain, unsparing, and heartrendingly poignant."   —*Daily Mail* (UK)

For *Crongton Knights*

"Has 'classic' singing from every page . . . Wheatle's Twain-like command of patois never falters . . . Enriching and life-affirming . . . A total gem for any age." —*Independent* (UK)

"Elegant, authentic, and humane. It hums with the beat of real life and the language sings from the page. This is mature, powerful writing by an author with great talent and great heart."
—David Almond, author of *The Colour of the Sun*

"A fast-paced, funny ride." —*Metro* (UK)

"Funny, profane, well-observed accounts of life on an urban estate."
—*Sunday Times* (UK)

"Continual banter is laced with excellent near-the-knuckle jokes . . . this story, which never lets up . . . has much of value to say."
—*Books for Keeps* (UK)

"Brilliant, tough, heart-breaking read." —Tanya Landman,
author of *Buffalo Soldier*, Carnegie Medal winner

For *Liccle Bit*

"A gripping tale of family and friends, love and loyalty."
—Malorie Blackman, author of *Noble Conflict*

"My favorite book of this season . . . sings with warmth in spite of its tough setting . . . a gritty delight—a liccle smile on every page."
—*Sunday Herald* (UK)

"Topical and also a triumph of language . . . Wise as well as witty, understanding rather than blinkered, this novel is a joy to read."
—*Independent* (UK)

CANE

WARRIORS

CANE
WARRIORS

BY

ALEX WHEATLE

Published by Akashic Books
©2020 Alex Wheatle

Front cover photo: adapted from "Children in Birao 18" by hdptcar from Bangui, Central African Republic, commons.wikimedia.org. CC By-SA 2.0.

Hardcover ISBN: 978-1-61775-906-2
Paperback ISBN: 978-1-61775-855-3

Library of Congress Control Number: 2020935818
All rights reserved
First printing

Black Sheep
c/o Akashic Books
Brooklyn, New York
Twitter: @AkashicBooks
Facebook: AkashicBooks
E-mail: info@akashicbooks.com
Website: www.akashicbooks.com

**More books for young adult readers
from Black Sheep**

Home Girl
by Alex Wheatle

Around Harvard Square
by C.J. Farley

Game World
by C.J. Farley

Changers Book One: Drew
Changers Book Two: Oryon
Changers Book Three: Kim
Changers Book Four: Forever
by T Cooper & Allison Glock-Cooper

Broken Circle
by J.L. Powers and M.A. Powers

Pills and Starships
by Lydia Millet

The Shark Curtain
by Chris Scofield

This story is based upon true events. I dedicate it to the mighty Tacky and his fellow cane warriors of 1760, Toussaint L'Ouverture and his brothers who led the Haitian revolution in 1791, Fédon's 1790s slave uprising in Grenada, the 1816 slave revolt led by Bussa in Barbados, Sam Sharpe's Baptist War slave rebellion in Jamaica 1832, and to freedom fighters all over the world.

—*Alex Wheatle, South London*

1

A WHISPER IN THE NIGHT

Frontier Plantation, St. Mary, Jamaica, 1760

Sleep was hard to catch on this humid night. I was listening to the chanting of tiny creatures in the fields when I felt a strong palm on my shoulder. I turned my head and opened my eyes. Louis stood over me. His top garment, the sleeves rolled up above his elbows, was stained with soil. His eyes had a red fire in them. Sweat dripped off his chin. Through the open window I saw a fat moon—only days ago full fat. Its pale light reflected off Louis's forehead.

He bent down and whispered into my ear, "Moa, it's been agreed."

"What's been agreed?" I asked.

Louis checked around the small room. Ten men slept around me. There was no space to stretch or roll over. Two of them snored. Like me, they had worked fourteen-hour shifts cutting the cane. The endless cane. Like me, their bodies were spent and roasted by a brutal sun. Harvesttime was upon us. There'd be long days and weeks ahead of us.

Louis's thick fingers dug into my shoulder. I sensed the power in his forearms. I wanted to grow broad and strong like him. I hoped he could pass on his courage to me too. "We is going to bruk outta here 'pon what de white mon call Easter Sunday," he said. "T'ree days' time."

"White mon Easter Sunday?" I repeated. Something colder than blood flowed through my veins.

"Yes, mon, dem Easter Sunday," nodded Louis. "De men and women cyan't tek it no more. Not after Miss Pam drop inna de field and lose her life. Ever'body leggo some long-long eye-water. Me sure you eyes sore too. You know dat she was wid chile? Not even we gods—Asase Ya, Nyame, or Abowie—coulda save her. Who gonna tell de liccle pickney Anancy stories now? Dem should know dat Anancy de son of Asase Ya and Nyame. Scallion Mon and me had to dig de hole and dem just fling her inside it. Dem would not allow us to bury her beside ah tree or de stream. Not one Akan song chant."

I recalled the time when Miss Pam treated the blisters on my hands with some herbs she had boiled.

Mama said she had learned tings from the Akan elders. She helped deliver my little sister Hopie, and looked after Papa's wound when it became sore. We all loved her. Sadness shook my heart and rage filled my fists once again.

"She was good to ever'body," I said. "Dem never let me say goodbye to her."

Louis's eyes burned into me. "Moa, you understand dat if we bruk outta here, somebody have to kill off Misser Master and him wife and all de overseer dem."

My body begged for more rest but my heart punched rapid combinations. I felt the vibrations in my throat. "Do we really have to kill master wife too? Do we have to kill any of dem? We cyan't just run off in de nighttime?"

Louis shook his head. "We have to kill dem, Moa. Otherwise dem will send more white people to hunt we down. You nuh hear from you mama about how master's wife treat we people inna de big house?"

"Yes." I nodded. "Mama always complaining. Somebody get lash just becah dem drop some food. Sometime Mama nuh finish work till de bird sing inna treetop."

I had to take a moment. Louis, broad shoulders and thick leg-back, was one of the oldest men on the plantation. He was three years shy of forty. I was fourteen years old and my chances of counting my harvests to thirty-seven were slim like the weed leaf that children had to dig out from around the cane. Life was hard as a boy-child. But now that I had nearly come to my full size, my life was going to get tough like an old tree root.

"How?" I asked. "When?"

Louis glanced over his shoulder. The green things in the field continued their debate. The smell of crushed cane, boiled sugar, and smoke filled our nostrils. The mill never slept.

"As me just done tell you," Louis replied, "t'ree days' time—de white mon's Easter Sunday. Misser Master will give some of de white overseer de day off so dem cyan celebrate dis ting call Easter. Dem will be laughing and walking strange after dem drink de mad cane water. We have to tek we chance."

"Tacky going to lead we?" I wanted reassurance. "Me will feel ah whole heap better if he did. Him hand mighty and him have ah good head. Me mama say de gods walk wid him. She say him was born to back de evil against de wall."

"Yes, mon," Louis said. "Of course. Nuh forget, Miss Pam was Tacky's sister. Misser Master nuh even know dat. Tacky has to play dis pretend game becah he has to gain de trust from Misser Master. Sometimes you have to play fool to get wise. And Tacky playing it good. Tacky still remember de land at de other end of de blue waters. *Dreamland* him call it. Him still remember some words and ways dat de white mon nuh know about. Him cyan say someting right in front of Misser Master dat is ah message to we."

"Tacky have one fierce strong back," I said. "Me glad he will lead we."

"Moa, catch some sleep," Louis instructed. "You going to need it. Me will come tomorrow and give you more news. Nuh chat to nobody of dis except me—not even you papa."

Louis checked the men around me before he left for his own hut. I peered out the window and he became a shadow in the steamy Jamaican night.

I thought of my father and hoped I'd see him in the morning when he finished his shift at the mill. I tried to guess how many moments of rest I could claim before the sun walked in the sky again. My limbs became weary as I thought about the day's work ahead. I closed my eyes as my head hit the dusty floor.

The snorers continued.

2

CUTTING THE CANE

Miss Gloria wasn't smiling today. She dipped her spoon into the big cornmeal pot and served breakfast to the men. "Me glad you still living," she said to Toolmon, the gray-bearded man who repaired and sharpened billhooks and other instruments we used in the field. She usually said her greeting with a grin. Not today. Maybe she missed Miss Pam too. Louis and the other elders had always instructed us not to "leggo eye-water" in front of the white overseers. *Nuh let de white mon see de pain you carry inside.*

When it was my turn to be provided, Miss Gloria offered me a quick glance. Her eyes were sore but her cheeks were dry. Misser Donaldson, a white overseer, looked on from his cabin veranda behind the cook-house. A wide hat topped his fair hair. It had a brown chicken feather sticking out of it. One side of his face was red with sunburn.

I sat down on the grass under the shade of a tree. I scraped every last drip of cornmeal into my mouth. It would be six hours before my next meal, usually a piece of salted pork and a scrap of bread at lunchtime. I glanced at the high green hills to the east and wondered what was on the other side. Maybe there was a land where there was no overseer or Misser Master. The Dreamland that Tacky talked about. Maybe there were green fields where mothers didn't have to toil in the fields and brothers weren't whipped if they caught long moments of rest in the late afternoon. *One day, me will have to tek me good foot and see wid me own eye. Yes, Moa. Mek me promise meself dat before me good body return to de ground.*

I looked around for Papa but couldn't spot him. I guessed he must be eating at another breakfast station near the millhouse. Keverton sat beside me. He was two thumbs taller than me, one branch wider, and two years older. He only had three fingers on his left hand after an accident with a billhook. His watchful eyes darted between me and Misser Donaldson.

"Moa, how are you arms keeping?" Keverton asked.

"Me nuh even know," I replied. "Sometimes, when me finish work it's like me have no arms at all."

Sometimes when the sun got tired for the day, it felt like the billhooks we carried were as heavy as a fat donkey. Sometimes when the sun climbed to the middle of the great sky, it felt like it was roasting every little hair on my head. I was surprised it didn't turn yellow. Sometimes when Misser Donaldson used his back-ripper on me, it felt like he was cutting cane from my body.

Keverton spied a quick look at Misser Donaldson again and dropped his tone to a whisper. "Did Louis talk to you last night?" he asked.

I didn't want to answer. Louis had warned me not to share any of Tacky's plans to anybody. Not even Keverton.

"Me nuh know what you talking about, Keverton."

"Moa, you cyan talk to me," Keverton assured. "Louis come to me last night too. On de white mon's Easter Sunday, we have ah big job to do."

"Louis never told me about any job," I said.

Keverton thought about something. "He didn't? You sure? You cyan talk to me, Moa. Me know de plan."

I turned to Keverton and gave him a long look. "You do?" I said. "Louis tell me not to leggo one word."

Keverton nodded. "And you did good."

"Him shoulda tell me dat you know about Tacky's plan too."

"Maybe he didn't want you to fill up you head about it and talk about it wid me too much," Keverton said. "Mek sure you nuh give Misser Donaldson any problem today or tomorrow."

"Me nuh give Misser Donaldson any problem for ah long while," I said. "Me cut plenty-plenty cane since harvest start."

"Good," said Keverton. "Keep it up. Me nuh want him to suspect ah damn ting." He tipped the corn-meal into his mouth and stood up. "Come, mon. Let we start early today."

We placed our bowls into a wooden box beside Miss Gloria's serving station—later on she would take them down to the river to wash them. Her usual morning smile still hadn't reached her lips. I guessed Miss Pam's kind face was still behind her eyes. I felt the rise of eye-water but I managed to hold it back.

Keverton and I made our way to the cane field. We were the first to arrive. The sun had just peeped its crown over the eastern hills. There were no white puffs in the blue sky. We picked up our billhooks from a sack and started work.

We hacked the cane from about six inches above the ground and then chopped the leaves from the top. I gazed ahead and the pale stalks stretched out until they reached the horizon. My back already ached just above my behind and my palms were as hard as the dried mud. A few naked pickney had already started pulling and picking out the weeds. I remembered when I filled my long days with that chore. It seemed like play when I first began—until the overseers warned us we had to do the same thing every day, every week, until the moon turned skinny and got fat again.

"Dis is harder work than planting time," Keverton said. "Me just cyan't tek de smell of de cow and donkey shit Misser Master tell we to use to mek de cane grow."

"Me cyan't tek de bending down, standing up, and de bending down again," I said. "It's ah wonder me back nuh bruk yet."

"It *will* bruk if we nuh mek we move," replied Keverton.

I checked behind me and Misser Donaldson hadn't yet arrived on his donkey to check us. "What's dis job dat we have to do?"

"Louis will tell you tonight," Keverton said. "Me sure of dat."

"Why cyan't you tell me?" I urged.

More men had arrived for work. None of them looked forward to their day. Women and young girls pulled handcarts. They stopped here and there to pick up the fallen cane. They dragged it up the dirt path to the mill where it would be crushed. A dark smoke snorted out of the boilerhouse.

"It's not for me to tell you," Keverton finally replied. "Louis or Tacky have to do dat."

"Is it ah dangerous ting we have to do?"

I had a very good idea what my task was. I hoped Keverton said it was something different. He stopped cutting and stared into the field before he turned to me. He nodded. "Everyting is dangerous here, Moa. Even living till de next day. Even sleeping. Nuh ask me no more question. Just concentrate on you work while de sun walks de sky. Louis did ah warn me dat you will fling plenty question my way."

"But me have to know what kinda job dem want me to do," I said. "Me have to prepare me—"

A shooting pain spread from the top of my left shoulder down to my waist. I spun around and saw Misser Donaldson astride his donkey. I didn't hear him approach. His hat shadowed his forehead and his right hand twirled his back-ripper. It was whispered that it was part bull's tail, with hog bone and goat hide. I remembered what it had felt like when I had been "seasoned"—given my first lashes, no more than two moon cycles gone—and I had seen what it had recently done to Keverton as a punishment. It was one of the worse whippings we had seen. His back showed ridges of hard dried blood.

Misser Donaldson's teeth were as dirty as the manure banking and his ginger beard had specks of gray in it. Hate rippled through me. His red neck was ripe for strangling. My fingers wanted to wreak revenge but I gripped the sides of my coarse pants instead.

"You can't work so hard when you talk," he said. "Work!"

He slapped his donkey on its neck with his back-ripper and moved on. In the distance, I spotted Misser Bolton, the other overseer on our section. He was already flogging somebody. Keverton turned away from me, gripped his billhook, and chopped the cane in front of him. He didn't say another word until we stopped for our next meal.

Could we really and truly tek dem on?

I wanted to hear Tacky's voice reassuring me. I *needed* to see him.

3

PAPA

We finished our hard labor more than thirteen hours later. Every muscle in my back screamed. I couldn't feel my arms and I believed my kneecaps were about to drop off. The sun had cooked my headtop and somebody could have made a hot drink with my sweat.

Keverton and I made our way to Miss Gloria's serving station. She dipped her wooden spoon into a barrel of warm water and served us two cups. We drank underneath a tree as the sun turned amber.

"Me nuh know if me cyan mek it back to me hut," Keverton said. "Maybe dis Jesus who Misser Master talk about cyan give me ah new body when me wake up inna de morning."

"Me nuh want ah new body," I replied. "Me want ah new life."

"Miss Pam used to mek ah bush tea to bring life back to tired leg," Keverton said.

"Yes," I nodded. "Me t'ink me mama learn from Miss Pam which leaf she have to pluck."

Keverton sipped his water and switched a hard gaze on me. "How many times do me have to tell you, Moa? Be careful how you pass on knowledge. Misser Donaldson nuh like dat, and him have plenty spy. Nuh let you mout' run away from you. Keep it low. You nuh know who's listening."

Misser Donaldson was nowhere to be seen so I wondered why Keverton was so cautious. Maybe it was because during his seasoning two years gone, he had suffered more lashes than anybody. His back was crisscrossed with thick pinky-red scars under the recent blood. He always slept on his stomach.

"Me going to see Papa," I announced.

"Do you have to?" asked Keverton.

"Yes, me have to."

"Nuh keep him from him work," Keverton warned. "And nuh stay too long inna de millhouse or otherwise dem will mek sure you do ah shift there tonight."

Hamaya, determination printed on her forehead, struggled up the hill with her handcart full of cane. It made a rattling sound as she went on her way. The ruts in the dirt path were deep, and the loose wheels wobbled. I decided to help her—she was only eleven years old. It was just a few weeks ago that Misser Master gave her a dress and an apron to wear. Her shoes were too big for her. She had been blessed with generous lips and her keen eyes never missed a bird in the sky. She grinned at me before checking ahead for any overseers. There wasn't any in sight. Apart from Miss Gloria, only pickney had smiles on the plantation. I wondered for how long Hamaya would keep hers.

Sometimes, just before the sun took its sleep, the white men returned to their huts to eat, drink, and, after taking their pick, be with our young black women. I prayed to the Akan gods that Hamaya wouldn't suffer that fate.

"Moa," she said, "you too good to me, but nuh let Misser Berris sight you wid me. He will find plenty extra work for you to do."

"Nuh worry youself, Hamaya. Let me help you up de hill."

We reached the top of the rise and I took a moment to gaze at the green mountains in the east. They promised freedom and adventure. I could almost hear them calling me.

Hamaya watched me. "You always looking 'pon de green mountains," she said. "Maybe one day you cyan tek me to de other side."

I laughed. "Maybe when you grow to you size."

Hamaya pulled out her defiant face. "Me grow to me size already and me foot strong."

"Yes," I agreed, "me notice."

"And Misser Berris and some of de other slave-master notice too." Her head dropped. She stared at the ground. "Dem will soon come for me, Moa," she said. "Sometime me hear de fussing and fighting and cussing from de white mon hut. When de women come back, dem nuh know which way to look. Nobody say ah damn word till de morning come. Me nuh want dat, Moa."

Hamaya lifted her head. Her expression was sad but strong. Her gaze went right through me. I knew she was pleading with me to do something. Anything.

I couldn't meet her eyes. I wished she could have stayed five or six forever, with a broad grin blessing her cheeks as she ran through the plantation.

I had to look away.

I wondered in what direction lay the wide blue waters. A little farther up the path was the big house. Field slaves like me were forbidden to plant one toe near there. My mama cooked in the big kitchen behind the mansion. She had to rise two hours before the sun woke to prepare the fires in the oven. She had to serve Master's wife and her children knowing that one dropped spoon, a word out of place, or a long stare could mean a lashing. She didn't take her rest until the last dinner plate was scrubbed clean. I couldn't remember her ever preparing a meal for me. The last I saw of her was three full moons ago.

We approached the entrance of the mill and tipped our load near the piles of cane that were stacked outside. The bundles were taller than two of me. Little Johnny, eight years old, ran over with a small stepladder, picked up our cane, and placed it on top of the stack. He secured it with twine. Hamaya started back down the hill. I wondered how many times she made that trip every day. She paused for a short moment and glanced at the green hills again. *Dem will soon come for me, Moa.* Her words wouldn't let me go. At least my terror was only during the day. *Maybe she dreaming de same dream dat fill up me head ah nighttime.*

I saw my papa and stood watching him feed the cane into the rollers. I hardly saw him do anything else. It made an ugly sound. He was a thumb taller than me but he seemed small. I used to have dreams of him leading me up into the hills. But not anymore.

Another man, Mooker, led a donkey that was tied to a rope attached to the wide wooden wheels. The cane juice was caught in a giant bowl built into the ground.

I approached my father. "Papa."

He didn't turn round. He continued pushing the

cane into the rollers with his one hand. Since he lost his left arm he wouldn't turn to look at anyone while he was working. "Moa? Is what you doing here?"

"Long time me nuh see you," I said.

"De time will be longer if Misser Berris find you foolish self here."

Mooker stole a quick glance at me before looking away. He was the one who hacked my father's arm off with an ax when it got caught in the rollers. This act saved Papa's life. The wooden machinery was still stained red. I couldn't imagine the agony Papa suffered. The donkey plodded on, its nose close to the ground. Barefoot, Mooker didn't care when he trod in the animal's shit.

"Me did want to see you," I said. "Louis come visit me last night."

Papa glanced at me over his shoulder. I could tell he didn't like my news. "Louis come to see you last night?"

"Yeah, mon," I replied.

"Did he talk him dangerous talk?"

I nodded.

Papa dropped his tone to a whisper. "Me know dem talking about ah bruk-out, but listen to me good, Moa. You cyan't go wid dem."

"Papa, me have to go wid dem. Louis expect me to go."

"Better if you stay here and live." Papa glanced at me once more. "Dem will cramp you. And dem will kill you slow by starving you inna cage. Dem will bring liccle pickney to see you. De same ting happen to me brudder. When him dead, he was not'ing more than de branches of ah maaga tree."

"Dem cyan't starve we if we kill dem first," I replied.

Papa shook his head before concentrating on feeding the rollers again. "You your mama's and me first-born. De toilet sickness tek Namoro two harvesttime ago. Bokara never even get to see five full moons."

"Me know dat, Papa, you nuh have to remind me."

"Then you cyan't go wid dem, Moa. Dem will ask me to dig you pit. And dat will tek plenty time wid me one hand. And dem will mek ever'body see it up by de long post by de big house. Dem love to give de good people of de plantation ah warning."

"Me mek up me mind, Papa," I said. "Me nuh want to let Louis and Keverton down. No, mon. Better me dead fighting than dead from working for de white mon. So many of we are tired of meking dem belly fat. Misser Donaldson back-ripper might send me to de pit tomorrow anyway."

Papa shook his head again. "Then me have lost another son. You t'ink me want to see all me bwoy-chile dead-off before me? No, Moa!"

"Me might live," I said. "And reach de other side of de green mountains."

"You better not stand up here for too long," Papa said. "Misser Berris will soon come and him love him back-ripper more than him love to drink de mad cane water."

"You could come wid we. You want to dead here so? By your rolling machine?"

He dropped his gaze and stared at the ground. "Me will keep me good foot here," he said. "If me get de chance, me will talk to Louis about his dangerous talk. He will get de sons of good people like meself killed for true."

I searched his eyes for a short while before I left. Papa had fed those rollers since before I was born. Maybe he would die there.

At the bottom of the hill I spotted Misser Berris. His garments couldn't contain his belly and he sweated under his hat. His cheeks were sun-kissed red. For a short moment I imagined him coming for Hamaya next time the moon was full fat. A bubbling hatred burned within me.

Papa only had three days of recovery when he lost his arm. Misser Berris refused to grant him an easier job like planting vegetables near the big house or caring for animals. I kept to the edge of the dirt track and hoped he wouldn't notice me.

"Guinea bird," he called me. His back-ripper was tied to his trouser belt. He hooked his thumb around it. "What are you doing in the millhouse?"

"Me . . . me was helping liccle Miss Hamaya, Misser Berris. She . . . she did drop her load. So me help her put de cane back inna de cart."

Misser Berris gave me a long suspicious glare before striding up the hill. I breathed an easy breath and went on my way.

"Guinea bird!" Misser Berris called me again.

I turned around. Something plowed in my belly. I remembered what Louis advised: *Bow you head ah liccle and nuh look de white mon in de eye.* I recalled the lashing he gave to Pitmon only two weeks ago. Till there was hardly any skin left on Pitmon's back. Misser Berris had to shake his back-ripper plenty times and dip it into warm water to get rid of Pitmon's flesh. Then Keverton was ordered to dig his hole. A silent fury echoed around the plantation that night. Nobody slept. "Yes, Misser Berris?"

"Make sure you go to the hut and get your sleep," he said. "We don't want any tired guinea birds in the morning."

"Yes, Misser Berris," I replied. "Me going to catch some sleep now after me get ah liccle someting to eat."

I stopped by Miss Gloria's food station and she

served me some chicken-back bones to gnaw on with cornmeal. I washed it down with water as the moon came out with its full face beginning to hide. By the time I arrived at my hut, eight men and two boys younger than me were already sleeping. I took my position on the floor and slumber claimed me quick. My dreams imagined the mysterious side of the green mountains and fat chickens.

4

THE JOB

Louis shook me awake. I opened my eyes and he pressed a broad finger to his lips. He peered out of the window and we could see the tops of the trees dimly lit by the plump moon. Mosquitoes buzzed around us. "Come, mon," Louis said. "Let we step outside."

I followed him through the door and we made our way to a tall tree. We sat down, resting our backs against the trunk. The insects in the fields were mighty loud this night. Strange birds squawked their squawks. Louis looked here and there before he spoke. We heard the distant crunching from the millhouse. "Moa," Louis started, "you body good?"

"What do you mean if me body good?"

"You cyan't bruk out if you cyan't run good or if you cyan't kill ah white mon when you need to."

I swallowed spit, gazed into Louis's eyes, and said, "Me body good, mon. Me cyan run as far as me need to and me cyan kill ah white mon. Me nuh have no problem wid dat."

I did have a problem with that. *Could me really kill ah white mon?*

"Dat is what me want to hear," said Louis.

"What is me job?" I wanted to know.

Louis checked over his shoulders. No one was about. I guessed there were overseers patrolling near the entrance of the plantation at the bottom of the hill. We couldn't see them.

"Your job," Louis said, "and Keverton's job is to kill Misser Donaldson on Sunday night just after de sun drop."

I didn't reply. It felt like those big wooden rollers that Papa feeds the cane into were now grinding in my belly. Sweat drowned my face. My pulse banged my temples.

"Use your billhooks," Louis continued. "Aim straight for de gut or de chest. Use two hands and dig deep. And then twist it like you meking ah fire. Mek sure he nuh breathe one dutty breath again."

It took me awhile to answer. *Kill Misser Donaldson?* I guessed he might've asked me to run somewhere when de bruk-out start. My heart kicked my ribs and didn't stop.

"But we have to put dem inna de sack when we finish work," I pointed out.

Louis shook his head. "Not on Sunday you won't."

Sunday was only two dawns away.

Papa would never agree. He would say it's not worth the agonies that will come to you.

But Pitmon never raised a hand or a fiery tongue to anyone until Misser Master troubled his daughter.

And Miss Pam was like a second mama to everybody but they just flung her in the pit after she dropped.

Me must lend me good foot and hand to de cause.

"Who's going to kill Misser Master?" I asked.

Louis took his time in answering. "Tacky," he said. "Everyting start when de sun tek cover behind de hills."

"Me will dig Misser Master hole wid me own hands if me have to," I said. "And fling him inside wid plenty chicken claw."

"There will be no time to dig anyting," Louis said. "We have to forward on quick-time to Fort Haldane. It's by de blue waters. Tacky say dem have guns there."

"Guns?" I repeated. "Dem tings dat fire quick deat'? Me remember me papa talk about it one time."

Louis nodded. "Yes, mon. Dat is de plan. Now, return to you hut and catch some sleep."

"Me cyan't sleep now, Louis," I said. "Me head full of tomorrow's worries and de day after."

"Me too," Louis admitted. "Try to empty you head and sleep good."

"Not yet," I said. "De inside of me head nuh tired yet."

"Then at least let you good body rest. It deserve dat."

"No, Louis. Me have to see me mama."

Louis shook his head. "Dat is outta de question. We cyan't have any field slave going up to de big house—"

"Louis," I interrupted, "me might not bless me eyes 'pon her again. Me want to say goodbye to her and me liccle sister Hopie."

"If you get catch, Misser Master will ask why you want to see her 'pon dis night. And even if you give ah good answer, he will whip you for true."

"Me won't get catch, Louis. Me know de back way. Me know de hut where Mama sleeping."

Louis thought about it and then shook his head again. "Tacky won't like it. No, mon, me cyan't let you do dis."

"Louis, you mama dead and gone long time," I said. "And when she drop down you never get ah chance to say goodbye to her. If you could tek back dat time, wouldn't you want to say ah liccle someting to her?"

Glancing up to the heavens, Louis then closed his eyes. He looked like he was remembering something. He mumbled a few Akan words that I couldn't understand. "All right," he said, opening his eyes. "If you get catch and Misser Master draws for him back-ripper, you nuh know anyting about we bruk-out plan. You understand? If you tell him anyting, me will kill you meself."

Louis's eyes captured me and wouldn't let me go for a long moment.

Misser Master's back-ripper was long. Some said it was made of bull hide, bark slices, and horse neck bones. He also secured it to his belt and it dangled near to his feet.

"Me understand," I said. "Me have to see her."

"And one more ting," said Louis. "If you get catch and Tacky ask question, me never give you no permission to go up to de big house. You understand?"

"Yes, mon, me understand."

Louis checked this way and that and vanished into the Caribbean night.

5

MAMA

I sat down for a long while and closed my eyes. I imagined plunging my billhook into Misser Master's chest. I saw the blood gushing out of his torso. I had seen many dead black bodies but I was yet to see the death mask of a white man. *Could me really tek de last breath of one of dem? Do dem bleed red like we? When dem dead, do dem eyes look like somebody steal de light of dem?*

I took a few moments to steady my nerves before starting for the bush. I used my fingers to climb up a steep bank. Twice I slid back down but I managed to secure a footing and pull myself up. I could see the fire lamps of the big house and outhouses through the trees and undergrowth. I had to lie very flat and still in the long grass as two overseers went by below me. I recognized one of them: Misser Penceton, he was the chief overseer and he lived in a big cabin forty steps away from Misser Master's big house.

I tried to control my breathing. They paused for a bit, talking about their homeland, the big mansions they wanted to build, and the women they wanted to marry. If they glanced up for one short moment then I'd be flogged by the tall post at the top of the hill where everyone could see. Misser Master enjoyed spectacles like that.

I thought about crawling back and returning to my hut. But I had made it so far. I had to see Mama. Finally, the two men strolled on.

I skirted the front lawns and vegetable plots of the mansion where Tacky did his work. I crept by the overseers' huts before sliding down a dry muddy slope that led to a gully. A stream cut a jagged path through the hard earth. I took a moment to drink and wet my face. It was refreshing and cool. The pit toilet was dug nearby and the stench filled my mouth, nostrils, and chest. The house-slave huts were placed beyond the pit toilet next to the hog pen. I heard the cocks cluck-clucking in the distance. For a moment the idea of stealing a chicken entered my head—my mouth watered—but I thought better of it. I made my way to the third hut of five and tapped on the open window. It was dark inside. "Mama!"

No response.

A baby cried in the end cabin. A mother sang Akan words to it.

"Mama," I called, this time a little louder.

I heard somebody climbing to their feet. I hoped they hadn't moved her.

"Moa? Ah you dat?"

"Yes, Mama."

"Hold on ah liccle."

"Is dat Moa outside?" another voice asked. It was Hamaya. She had shared my mother's house-slave cabin since her parents died. I wondered for how long Misser Masser would allow her to sleep there. "Cyan me see him?"

"No, Hamaya," replied Mama. "It best if you try catch sleep again."

"But me want to see him."

Mama didn't respond.

"By de next fat moon dem might come for me, Moa," called out Hamaya. "Dem cyan't do anyting to me if me was by de dark side of de tall hilltop."

"Hush you mout'," scolded Mama.

Hamaya's words tore into my chest. *But me job is to kill Misser Donaldson, not to tek Hamaya's good hand and lead her to de other side of de long mountain.*

I strained my eyes into the night, trying to check for any sign of overseers. All seemed well. Mama emerged out of her cabin. "Come, Moa," she said.

"We'll talk beside de pit toilet—de white mon nuh go near there."

"De flies nuh mind," I said.

Mama aimed her words into her hut: "Hamaya, stay where you be. *Nuh* follow we."

"Where's Hopie?" I asked.

"She sleeping," Mama replied. "Me nuh want to wake her. She might get ah liccle excitable and holler and scream when she sight you. De same could be said for Hamaya. She really sweet 'pon you."

I followed Mama to the pit toilet. The stink filled my nose and I almost sneezed. Flies hummed above our heads. Mama smiled and gave me a quick hug.

"Me should really beat de good sense back into you!" she said. "If Misser Master or Misser Penceton catch you here, you back will taste de ripper again. You nuh have no good sense, Moa?"

"Me had to see you, Mama."

Her tone was angry. "Why?"

Mama was sweating. Maybe not from the humidity but from the worries she always carried, though she had kind eyes still. A white head-rag covered her hair. Her fingers were broader than mine and the night garment she wore was thick. Nothing covered her hard feet.

I took a deep breath. "We're going to bruk outta

here 'pon Easter Sunday—when de sun tek ah dip."

My mother thought about it. I expected her to disapprove just like Papa.

"Ah true?" she said. Hope was in her voice.

"Yes, Mama, ah true."

She swatted a fly and seized me with her eyes. She grabbed my shoulders and I felt the strength of her grip. "You have me blessing," she said. "Tek you good foot and leave dis land. Never come back."

"Me was t'inking dat you and Hopie would come wid me," I said.

Mama laughed. "Ah crazy talk you ah talking! How is me old foot and liccle Hopie going to keep up wid you and fight de white mon?"

"But Mama . . . me nuh want to leave you here—"

"Listen me good, Moa. Me nuh want you to fill you head wid Hopie and me. You must forget about we. Nuh you t'ink dat after you gone me will smile at nighttime? And me will say to meself at least one of me pickney leave dis wicked place. And maybe he be at someplace better. Me have to believe dat better must come for you. You must leave me wid dat hope inna me head."

"But Mama—"

"Talk no more, Moa. You must do what you have to do. You nuh t'ink Miss Pam ever dream of her sons escaping from dis place? She never live to see it. Me want to live and hear de story and me will tell de tale to liccle Hopie."

"Me hear Louis talk about dis Dreamland," I said. "And Tacky too."

"Nuh worry you pretty liccle head about Dreamland," said Mama. She fixed a hard stare on me. "Just tek you swift foot and go'long from dis wicked place."

"But me might not see you again, Mama."

She thought about it and wiped the sweat from her forehead. "And dat will be ah good ting."

"Ah good ting?" I repeated.

"Yes, mon," Mama said. "Why do you t'ink Miss Gloria smile and show her good teet' every morning?"

"Me nuh know, Mama."

"Becah her eldest son Midgewood mek him escape."

"Me never know Miss Gloria had ah son call Midgewood."

"Yes, mon," Mama confirmed. "Him now twenty-t'ree years old. None of we talk about it becah Misser Master get vex when he hears him name. And Misser Master tell Misser Penceton dat dem must whip anybody who mention him name. Midgewood was broad and strong. One time me overhear Misser Master saying him was wort' ah whole cartload of money. But Midgewood lef' and gone and dat's why Miss Gloria smile ah morning time."

"She nuh smile dis morning," I pointed out.

"Dat's becah of Miss Pam," Mum explained. "Ever'body's heart well heavy like fat donkey back-side wid dat news. Plenty eye-water ah fall. She was ever'body's mama."

"Louis and plenty other mon want to tek dem revenge," I said.

Mama thought about it. "Good!"

I gazed into her eyes. It might be the last time I look into them. "So me have you blessing?"

Tears rolled down Mama's cheeks. She cradled my jaw with both hands. It felt good to feel her touch. Suddenly her eyes came alive. "Run, Moa! Nuh turn back! Look for Midgewood if you cyan. Mek me smile every morning when me there inna de cookhouse or de smokehouse. And when Misser Master's wife cuss me and bruk her hand across me face if de dinner nuh cook right. Sometime me so tired, sleep catches me when me stand up and stir de big pot. And it so damn hot inna de cookhouse dat me surprise me nuh look like roast hog. But if you run away, dat will give me plenty hope."

"Me will try me best, Mama."

"Yes, Moa. And when you gone me going to tell liccle Hopie about you. Yes, mon. Misser Master have dis big book inna de big house. Me see Misser Master pickney reading it. Me want to teach liccle Hopie to read and write so she cyan tell we story."

"Nuh let Hopie forget me," I said.

"Me won't," Mama replied. "Now, tek you good foot and go back to you own hut. Be careful. De overseer dem sometimes walk at strange times under de broad moon."

"Nuh worry, Mama," I said. "Me know de back way where de white mon bad toe nuh tread."

We hugged quickly.

Before I started, I concentrated my ears and peered into the blackness around me. "Let Asase Ya smile 'pon you, Mama."

"Ah! You remember we mama god." She smiled. "Let she protect you too and nuh let you pickney forget her."

"Me won't, Mama."

I turned. My first few steps were short.

"*Kwan so dwoodwoo*," called Mama.

I didn't face her. I stood still. "What does dat mean, Mama?"

"Safe travel."

6

LOOSE TALK

made my way back to my place of rest undetected. I heard a fierce argument coming from behind Keverton's hut. I recognized Papa's voice and ran down the hill. About fifty steps away from the last field-slave cabin, Keverton, Louis, and Papa cursed each other. Their hand-pointing and gestures were fiery. A horrible feeling whipcracked through me. They spotted my approach and stilled their tongues as if nothing had happened. None of them wanted to look at me.

"Even de lizard 'pon Misser Master veranda ah hear you cuss-cussing," I said. "Stop you noise! You want to wake up de whole plantation?"

Louis gave Papa a blazing eye-pass. Keverton shook his head.

Papa returned Louis's glare with a fierce look of

his own. "You cyan't tek him wid you," he said to Louis. "Me won't let you take him wid you!"

"Moa already mek up him mind," Louis argued.

"Moa cyan talk for himself," I said. "And me give me good word, me hand, and me foot to Tacky cause. It nuh just Tacky cause no more. It's de whole ah we. From Mama, Hamaya, and ever'body else. Dem me ah fight for."

"Him too young," Papa protested as he stamped a foot. "Just ah few moons ago, Moa was picking out de weeds inna cane field. Just de other skinny moon, Misser Donaldson season him. Him back only just heal. He's him mama last bwoy-chile—"

"Papa," I cut in, "yes, me cyan't lie. Me t'ought me was going to dead when me get season and it still pain me when me roll 'pon me back. Sometime when me sleeping me see Misser Donaldson back-ripper talking to me. But Mama give me her blessing. Me going wid dem for true. Everyting set up. Me have ah job to do."

Papa switched his gaze from Louis to Keverton. His jaw muscles twitched. I felt the tension in my throat. Papa seemed to know what "job" meant. "You cyan't ask him to do dat," he objected. "Moa will get kill-off before Tacky bruk-out even start."

"Me have to do me job, Papa," I said. "Me cyan't back out. No, mon. If me back out, in plenty years to come, we blood won't remember me."

"Then you leave me wid no choice," Papa said. "Me will tell Misser Master meself. Me cyan't just stand up and do not'ing when me first-born walking to him foolish deat'. It's better dat Tacky, Louis, or anyone else dead before you."

It happened so quick. Louis rushed up to Papa, swung a fist, and sent him flying to the dirt. Papa pushed himself up with his one arm and kicked out at Louis. Louis levered a punch from way behind his back. It lifted Papa off the ground. I squinted as he landed with a solid thud. Invisible lashes split my heart every time they thumped each other. I thought my head was going to burst like a coconut being crushed by a wooden mallet.

"Me will *kill* you for dat!" raged Papa.

"Stop it, mon!" I yelled. "Stop it!"

Louis leaped on top of Papa and strangled him with his big hands and thick forearms. Papa croaked and gasped for breath. I saw the pain in his eyes. He glared at me. I found it hard to meet his gaze. Louis squeezed harder. I stepped forward a pace. Then another. I clenched my hands into fists.

I couldn't take it anymore. I ran to try to intervene but Keverton stepped in front of me. He raised his hands and challenged me. He pushed out his chin and narrowed his eyes. *How cyan me fight Keverton? He's my brudder. My teacher.*

"If we let him go," Keverton said, "you papa's tongue could send ah whole heap ah we brudders to de pit. Moa, me beg you. Remember Pitmon."

I relaxed my fingers.

Louis increased the pressure on Papa's neck. Papa coughed and spluttered again. His eyes bulged like a sick donkey's. His one arm flailed up and down. He tried to pull Louis off of him but Louis was too powerful. Pitmon grew big in my mind yet I had to do something . . .

I evaded Keverton and ran five paces toward Papa.

A voice cut through the night from farther down the hill: "Animals!"

It was Misser Donaldson. He was accompanied by Misser Bolton. The grinding sensation returned to my stomach. Louis jumped off Papa and stood very still to attention. Keverton did the same and I didn't twitch one little toe. Papa slowly climbed to his feet. He dusted himself off and stared at the ground.

Approaching Louis, Misser Donaldson measured his steps around him with his hands behind his back. "You again," he said. "What's this about?"

Louis didn't reply. Papa kept quiet.

"What's this about?" Misser Donaldson repeated, this time louder. He reached for his back-ripper. On this night it seemed longer and coarser.

I tried to keep still but my heart boomed so hard it almost made me keel over.

"Just . . . just ah liccle argument about . . . about food," Louis managed.

Misser Donaldson lashed Louis across his face. The whipcrack sent birds flapping above. Eyes peered out of hut windows. Whatever lurked in the bush sprang away. Louis's face swelled up immediately, leaving an ugly red welt from the corner of his top lip to the edge of his left eye. Blood ran over his strong chin. The lash must've notched his cheekbone but Louis hid his pain well.

"Too many times I find you out at night," Misser Donaldson warned. "If you harm or stop one of our slaves from working, I'll get you to dig your own grave before I kill you myself. Umbassa may only have one arm but he's still worth ten pounds to his master."

Louis fixed his gaze to his feet. Blood dripped onto his footwear. "Yes, Misser Donaldson. It won't happen again, Misser Donaldson. Me sorry, sah."

Papa remained silent.

"All of you should be sleeping," Misser Donaldson said. "You always complaining how tired you are, so why aren't you sleeping?"

"Me . . . me was tending to Keverton arm," Louis lied. "Him was complaining about it today and he did want his arm to feel good by de morning so him cyan work good."

"Dat is true, Misser Donaldson," Keverton said. "Me arm and shoulder pain me since de last fat moon."

Misser Donaldson thought about it. I wondered if he'd fall for the old Jamaican slave trick—play fool and subservient to con the so-called wise. Misser Donaldson twirled his back-ripper and circled Louis once more. He then turned to Papa. "And what about you?"

I noticed Louis's eyes following Papa's every movement.

"Me . . . wanted to see me son, Misser Donaldson," Papa said. "It's . . . it's just de one son me have. So me was looking for him. Me wanted to teach him someting. Sometime him cut de cane too high. Me notice dat from me work at de millhouse. Misser Berris is always telling me dat we cyan't waste any of de good cane."

Misser Donaldson and Misser Bolton swapped doubtful glances.

"Go and get your sleep," Misser Bolton ordered. "You know the rules: three field slaves are forbidden to be abroad after sundown. Next time . . . you know what to expect."

I knew what to expect—a flogging while bound to the tall post outside the big house. Most boy-child my age didn't survive it. Pitmon didn't live after it. Misser Master ordered everybody to see Pitmon's dead body. They hung it up from a tree. He swayed gently in the breeze. They lashed him across the face so many times that he had no lips and just half a nose. His back didn't look like a back anymore—the color was scraped off. That same night Miss Pam sang an Akan song to try to soothe our hearts. Even Papa let go some of his eye-water. *Nuh go down Pitmon road*, Papa told me. *Me want you to live.*

"Yes, Misser Bolton," Keverton nodded. "It will never happen again."

Papa started up the hill. He didn't look back. His shelter was behind the millhouse. I made for my own hut, and when I found my place on the floor, I wondered if he really would reveal our bruk-out plans to Misser Master. *No*, I thought, *Papa wouldn't betray we like dat. Would he?*

7

PLAN FOR MURDER

The next day, the sun had just started to sink beyond the western hills when Keverton stopped work and gripped me with a stare. He hadn't spoken a word to me all afternoon.

"Moa," Keverton said. He looked this way and that for any sign of our overseer. "By dis time tomorrow, we'll be teking de light outta Misser Donaldson."

"Me know," I replied. "It's been 'pon me mind all day. And me couldn't sleep last night."

Keverton nodded. "Me too. Me been t'inking. We should just run into him cabin and jerk him up quick-time before him know what's going on. Better to get it over and done wid before we get too shaky-shaky."

I was shaky-shaky already. The cornmeal in my stomach decided to take the direct route to my throat. Then it went back down again. Papa's voice was echoing in a corner of my mind: *Nuh, Moa! Nuh kill any-one. Better if you stay here and live. Dem will cramp you . . . kill you slow by starving you inna cage . . .*

I took a few deep breaths. "Yes, mon," I managed.

"If luck shines 'pon we, Misser Donaldson will be teking him rest, lying down. And him have no god friend to tek him spirit to ah nice place."

"To know dat will mek tings easier." But I thought, *Not'ing will mek tings easier. Me wonder what we great mama god Asase Ya will t'ink of me after me kill ah mon.*

I resumed cutting the cane. Keverton had chopped so much more than me on this day and I hoped Misser Donaldson wouldn't notice.

"You," I stuttered, "you . . . you t'ink me papa say anyting to Misser Master?"

Keverton thought about it. "Me nuh t'ink so," he replied. "If he did, we all would've been lashed outside de big house by now."

"You t'ink me should go to me papa again and beg him not to say anyting?"

"No, Moa," Keverton shook his head. "Dem will t'ink someting going on. Louis say nobody is to go out tonight. Tacky's orders. Him nuh want any kind ah fuss or good people to get demselves inna big trouble. Not on dis night."

"Nobody?"

"Nuh bruk dat, Moa," Keverton said. "You like ah

brudder to me, Moa, but me will whip you meself if you go look for you papa tonight. As was said last night, there are too many good lives at stake. You understand?"

I wanted to try to convince Papa to come with us, but Papa's mind is hard to change, like hungry big-head mule who sight plenty grass.

I nodded. "Me understand. So . . . when we tek de billhooks after work, where we hide dem when we eating?"

"Miss Gloria have ah deep water pot," Keverton said. "So when we finish work, we drop de billhooks in there."

"But plenty people will see it."

"Misser Donaldson have him own water pot," said Keverton. "And more people now know about we bruk-out plan."

"Dem do?" I said.

"Yes, mon. You nuh know it but dis ting been plan long time. Some people are praying to de Akan gods for we victory. Good over evil dem ah pray for."

I felt a sharp wrench in my stomach again. "Even Miss Gloria know?"

"Of course she know. All we have to do is run into Misser Donaldson cabin, draw we billhooks, nuh give him time to even call we name, and tek him life. White mon cyan't survive ah long blade in dem belly no more than de black mon."

I closed my eyes and ran the scene over in my head. If we failed it'd be a long slow death strapped to that tall post outside the big house. *Dem might even put we inna cage and starve we to deat'. Dem might even force Mama to watch me breathe me last breath.* The thought of it shook my bones and roasted my cheeks. *Maybe Papa was right, me could end up dead before de bruk-out even start.*

"Everyting ready," Keverton said. "Ah whole heap ah we brudders and sisters are depending on we. Try and sleep good tonight, Moa. It'll be de last sleep you catch for ah long time."

8

SUNDIP TIME

White man Easter Sunday. An orange sun dropped to the west. I gazed at the rich green of the land. Much in the valleys was now cast in shadow.

I hadn't slept at all last night. The insides of my stomach had tossed and churned since I picked up my billhook for work. Keverton and I had cut as much cane as I could remember on this day. There were moments I just wanted to stop work and take my rest. Everything ached. Misser Donaldson went by on his donkey as the sun began to dip and nodded his appreciation. My blood seemed to bubble inside of me as he did so. I remembered my recent whipping. It wasn't the pain I recalled but the sound his back-ripper made. *Crack, poom. Crack, poom. Crack, poom.* I couldn't even glance at his boots let alone his face. His beast looked well tired. At least it didn't have blood ridges upon its back.

Miss Gloria had served us chicken wing and a bigger portion of cornmeal than usual for our midday meal. I threw most of it up a little later.

Keverton observed the skies. "It soon time, Moa."

I hoped the sun would get stuck in the sky. "Yes, me know."

"Let we wait till dem come and pick up de cane."

Moments later, Hamaya arrived with her wonky handcart. We helped her load it. She offered Keverton a smile but not me. Guilt lashed my insides. *Dem will soon come for me, Moa.*

"Why you nuh want to talk to me when you come up?" she asked me.

I guessed she was really asking me why I hadn't asked her to join the revolt.

"Me never had de time," I replied. "If Misser Penceton catch me up close to de big house then me back will get rip again for true. And he woulda mek you watch it."

Hamaya looked like she was deciding on my punishment, but eventually she grinned at me. "When you come up next time mek sure you talk to me. Remember, you de big brudder me never have." A sudden sadness shadowed her face. "There . . . there will be ah next time, Moa?"

It took me a long moment to answer. "Yes, there will be ah next time. Nuh worry you liccle self about dat."

"If someting happen, will you tek me wid you?"

I didn't want her to ask me this but she did.

"Not'ing happening, Hamaya," I lied.

She fixed me with a hard stare. "You sure?"

"Me sure."

When she set off, she turned to us and said, "May Amelenwa bless you good foot."

I remembered Miss Pam teaching us about Amelenwa—she was the goddess of rivers.

We watched her in silence as she struggled up the hill on the way to the millhouse. I wondered if Papa was about his work or if he walked up to the big house to reveal our bruk-out plan. When Hamaya disappeared from view, I searched Keverton's eyes. I wanted to see courage in them. "Are you ready?" I asked.

Keverton gripped his billhook. "Yes, me well ready. You hand strong?"

"Yes, me t'ink so," I said. "But me shaky-shaky inside."

"Dat nuh matter," Keverton said. "Just keep de shaky-shaky inside you belly. As long as you foot and hand strong."

"You back strong like de blue mahoe tree fighting de wind," I said to Keverton. "And you hand grip like de link of iron around new slave foot. Me glad me wid you."

"And me happy to be wid you. Nuh worry, Moa. We will finish we job."

"Me been t'inking," I said. "Say . . . say we rush in Misser Donaldson place and him not there? Him might be up by de big house."

"He'll be there," replied Keverton. "Him be up at de big house in de morning for white mon Easter breakfast or to pray to dem Jesus. Now he back and him always teking him rest when de sun sinking. Then him get up ah nighttime looking for mad cane water."

The shadows lengthened. Miss Gloria's food station was a few hundred yards up the dirt track. Today, it seemed a million miles away.

"Come, mon," Keverton said. "First ting we have to do is eat some food and drink ah liccle water."

Carrying our billhooks, we dragged one foot after another to Miss Gloria's serving counter. I guessed Keverton was just as tired as I was. When we arrived, we dropped our tools into the deep water pot. Other slaves watched us in silence as they licked their dishes and drank their water. Miss Gloria served us more chicken wing and chicken claw than usual with the cornmeal. She didn't utter a word but she looked up and smiled at us for a short second.

We made our way to the shelter of our favorite

guango tree to eat our meal. Keverton fixed his gaze on Misser Donaldson's hut, about thirty strides behind the open-air canteen. It had four wooden steps leading up to the front door. It had a wide veranda with two chairs sitting on it. The roof provided generous shelter for anyone who took their rest there. The windows were covered by white cloth. He had his own vegetable plot and pit toilet out back.

"Me hope he's in there," said Keverton.

"Me too. But me hope dat he's sleeping even more."

I licked my wooden bowl clean. Keverton drained the last drop of his water. He stood up first. "Come, Moa," he said. "De sun's taking its dip."

We dropped our bowls and mugs in the wooden box. Miss Gloria didn't meet our eyes. Fireflies hovered over her cooking pot. We collected our billhooks from the water tub. I sensed all eyes on me. I glanced up and down the dirt track. The western hills were now crowned with an amber glow. My heart pounded like Old Misser Cliff's hammer when he was fixing a large wheel. I shared a now-or-never look with Keverton. He nodded.

The small creatures in the field had already started their nighttime arguments. I gripped the handle of my knife so tight that redness appeared under my nails. Hamaya had stopped pulling her handcart on the way to the millhouse and watched us. I felt her eyes burning into me. *Dem will soon come for me, Moa.* It might be tonight they would drag her out of her cabin. If she refused they would take her anyway. I didn't want to fail her. My heart started to beat a warrior drum song. I prayed that the sky god Nyame would guide me.

Pickney stopped playing.

"Say . . ." I whispered to Keverton, "say de door bolted?"

"Bolted or not bolted, we have to kick it down."

And then Keverton dashed toward Misser Donaldson's hut. I soon caught up with him. If my heart could've run it would've reached the cabin first.

We both kicked the door down. Dust flew up in my eyes. I blinked furiously. Misser Donaldson was taking his rest on his bed. He only wore his pants. His chest and feet were bare. His back-ripper was on a table beside him next to an open bible and a wooden cup. He shot up quickly, not quite believing that he was being confronted by two field slaves armed with billhooks. He went for his back-ripper. Keverton hesitated. His weapon trembled in his right hand. I didn't want to see Keverton whipped again. I didn't want Misser Master to force me to view his broken body. I couldn't bear it to dig Keverton's pit. I didn't want to see him dangling from a thick branch. Fear left me. Nyame was with me.

I charged toward my tormentor.

The whipcrack was loud. He caught me on the neck and the pain was deep and intense. It didn't stop me.

Use both hands, Louis had advised. *Dig deep. Twist. Mek sure he nuh breathe another dutty breath.*

My aim was true. Just above his left nipple. My blade went in easier than I had imagined it. I turned the blade. He didn't scream. He just let out this long final breath. It was quite something watching the last moments of a dying man. He'd never enjoy a mug of rum again. No slave would ever feel the sting of his back-ripper. He'd never molest another Hamaya again. He'd never marvel once more at the red sun dipping beyond the western hills. I pulled my weapon out. He fell to the floor as did the bible. As I stood still, not believing what I had just done, Keverton leaped on Misser Donaldson and plunged his billhook into his back five times. The wooden floor turned red, staining the book. Some tiny ants scarpered, some got drowned in the blood. My heart thumped my rib cage. Keverton and I shared a look.

We heard screams and cries from outside. I pulled back the white cloth from the window. People ran here and there. All was chaos.

I looked at my fingers—they were soaked in blood. The white man bled just like we did.

"Come, Moa," Keverton urged. "We have to use we good foot and step it outta here."

I gazed at the body of Misser Donaldson once more. His fair hair was now painted crimson. His lips kissed the floor. Yes, I had stolen the light from his eyes.

"Moa!" Keverton raised his voice. *"Come, mon!"*

We dashed outside.

Misser Farridge, another overseer, was dragged out of his hut and hacked to death by Cornmon and Toolmon. Brothers and sisters hollered Akan war cries as mothers scooped up their young children and scampered to their cabins. Miss Gloria was nowhere to be seen.

Farther up the hill, rebels including Mooker— Papa's fellow worker at the millhouse—chopped Misser Berris's neck and torso. The slavemaster tried to flee but too many black hands wielded billhooks. He crumpled beneath the furious onslaught. He'd never take his stance again.

Papa wasn't in sight. For a short second I wondered if Mama and Hopie were safe. I considered running to them but I had given my good foot and hand to Tacky's rebellion.

"Moa!" Keverton hollered at me.

He yanked my arm and led me down the hill. I almost lost my footing in a deep wheel rut. We passed the lifeless body of Misser Bolton—his throat had been slashed and his face had been mutilated. It didn't seem real. I slowed my pace to check if it really was an overseer lying in the dirt. It was. My own blood cooked inside of me. Keverton had to pull me again.

We ran down the dirt path passing many slave cabins and work sheds. We made it to the front gate of the plantation. Seven white men were lying dead there too. I recognized the face of the overseer who was in charge of the stables. His head was almost decapitated. Keverton didn't allow me to pause and look at the corpses.

The dirt track bent and fell to the left, and the dark hills now appeared more menacing. Thick bushes bunched to our right. We finally stopped at a repair house not too far from the river. Old Misser Cliff, the wheelwright, spent his long days here. Broken wheels, carts, fence posts, and wooden tools surrounded us. More than thirty men had already reached the rendezvous point. All of them held a billhook or some other knife or weapon. I witnessed something I had never seen before—my brothers hugging and smiling at each other. A grin twitched the corners of my mouth.

Louis was also there. A thick scab ran across his face. He marched over to me looking as happy as I'd ever seen a black man. It was only now I realized that I had my own wound across my neck. It burned.

"All de overseer dem *dead*," Louis announced. "An' slavemaster Misser Berris. We just have to wait till Tacky reach to find out about Misser Master and Misser Penceton."

"Tacky nuh reach yet?" asked Keverton. He peered into the gathering gloom. "Maybe we go up and help him."

"No, mon!" Louis shook his head. "Tacky say for we to wait here so. Me nuh bruk dat."

There were a number of water jugs and urns in the outhouse. We refreshed ourselves and washed the blood off our hands and forearms. Minutes later, eight men arrived with vegetables, four goats, and three sackfuls of dead chickens. *"Awwurra!"* one of them cried.

"Awwurra!" we all repeated.

Louis strode toward me. "You done good," he said. "Me just hope dat Tacky done good too. Him strong like de trunk of ah blue mahoe tree. And him brain work quick like Anancy. Yes, mon."

9

TACKY

About half an hour later, we all stepped out of the shed and peered into the deepening night. The lamps in the big house still burned. A few stars appeared in the eastern skies. The chanting had faded and the cicadas and crickets seemed to cuss each other in the fields. The moon began its climb in the heavens. Louis walked up the dirt track and concentrated his eyes. "Me sight dem!" he exclaimed. "Me sight dem!"

I could make out six men emerging from the dark. Four of them carried a body. One of them pressed a rag to a wound he had sustained on his left shoulder. Somebody ran into the repair house to fetch a jug of water.

I hadn't seen Tacky for weeks. He wasn't that tall, not even that broad, but he trod like a king. He had intelligent eyes yet there was a ferocious determination behind them. He carried his chin high and when he spoke, every man present paid respectful attention. "Mek sure you bury Cudgemon outside de plantation area," he said to Louis. "Me nuh want him spirit to be chained here so. Let de trees overlook and guard him. Let him hear de skinny river rushing by. Mek sure you dig ah trench around de biggest tree and pour water and fruits in it. Dat will help we goddess, Bele Alua, find Cudgemon spirit and tek him away to we ancestors."

His voice was deep. It still retained an Akan tone. I couldn't recall Mama teaching me about Bele Alua. Maybe Miss Pam did talk about Her but I might not have paid attention.

"But bury him quick," Tacky added. "Me want to tek dis revolution to de Trinity plantation before de sun opens her eyes again."

Keverton and I relieved the men who carried Cudgemon's body. His corpse was still warm to the touch. We brought him beyond the plantation to a wooded area near the river. The ground was soft and yielding there. We dug a grave for him under the stars. We found the longest tree and carried out Tacky's orders. I then studied Cudgemon's face and thought of Papa's warning. *It could've been me. Maybe next time it will be me.* His body had two jagged holes in it. One in his neck and the other in his chest. The blood had dried and stained his top garment. He looked like he was enjoying a deep sleep. *Dead before de bruk-out even start.*

I closed my eyes. In my mind I saw Misser Donaldson's corpse. His mouth and his nostrils were perfectly still. My insides felt like a sharp piece of sugarcane was twisting through it. It almost made me sick. I wondered if Keverton felt the same way.

When we had finished digging, Keverton ran to fetch Louis, Tacky, and the others.

We all gathered around the grave. Mooker had now joined us. I looked at him. He shook his head in deep sorrow.

Tacky offered words to Nyame, Asase Ya, and Bele Alua. He chanted Akan phrases that I didn't understand. Old Misser Cliff chanted a lament.

It could've been me.

I didn't know Cudgemon, but an aching sadness rippled from my heart to the rest of my being. At least we had time to pay our respects and hand him over to the Akan gods and our ancestors. Misser Master never offered that courtesy for so many of our passed brothers and sisters. My blood remembered the murder of Pitmon and the death of Miss Pam. Hot revenge filled me up to my headtop.

As we filled the grave with good earth, I searched the eyes of my brothers. Renewed strength flowed through me.

To conclude the service, Louis tipped more water over Cudgemon's grave and into the trench around the long tree. "De blood remembers," he said.

"Tek rest, me brudders," Tacky ordered us. "Dem kill one of we, we will kill fifty of dem."

"Awwurra!"

We sat down. I couldn't pull my eyes away from Cudgemon's last resting place.

Tacky remained standing. "Misser Master dead," he told us. "And him woman and pickney. Misser Penceton's light is out too—we lef' him stinking body 'pon de front lawn. May de burning sun rot him where him lie."

"May de John Crow feed on dem bones for de longest time," added Louis.

"You kill de pickney?" Scallion Mon wanted confirmation. "You never tell we you were going to kill de pickney." Scallion Mon worked up in the fields beyond the big house planting vegetables. Miss Pam had raised him. He knew my mama but I hardly saw him.

Silence. A few of the men looked at each other. Some covered their mouths and whispered. Others stared at the floor.

"We goddess Abowie will nuh like dat," one said.

"None of we gods will like dat," added Scallion Mon. "Especially Abowie and Akonadi."

"You nuh t'ink dat when dem pickney grow to dem size dat dem won't whip you by de long post?" said Louis. "You nuh t'ink dem will kill you like dem did Pitmon? You t'ink when dem pickney grow dem will allow you to chant ah song when you dead?"

Doubt was in a number of eyes. Everyone muttered among themselves.

I spoke into Keverton's ear: "Me nuh t'ink me coulda raise me billhook and tek ah chile's life. No, mon. Me nuh t'ink me coulda do dat."

Keverton shook his head. I think he recalled his hesitation when he confronted Misser Donaldson. "Me nuh t'ink me could do dat neither," he admitted. "Me glad dat wasn't me job."

"Quiet, everyone!" Tacky shouted. The silence was immediate. "It had to be done. If we lef' dem alive dem foot and tongues coulda reach far. And when dem reach far dat could be de start of we doom. Dis way, we have more time to prepare."

"Before me leave dis place me going to pray to Bele Alua and give her what me cyan," said Scallion Mon. "Me want Her to look good on we."

"Me too," said another man.

"And me," nodded Keverton. He raised his hand. I wanted to hold up my hand too but thought better of it. I kept silent.

"We have no problem wid dat," said Louis. "Pray

you nice prayer. Bele Alua will bless you good foot."

Tacky approached each and every one of us and searched for the courage within our eyes. When he marched toward me, I felt my heart beat quicker. A sudden heat filled my head.

"When de sun is pulling on her boots and about to walk in de east," he said, "we'll help set we brudders and sisters free at de Trinity plantation. Dem know we coming. Remember, there are Miss Pams, Pitmons, Cudgemons, and we pickney there too."

"Awwurra!"

"Do we tek we rest here?" Louis asked. "Or go back to de wheelhouse?"

"Me want two mon to tek dem foot and go down de hill," Tacky said. "Me nuh want sleep to catch you yet becah me need you good eyes to check de dirt track. We kill off slavemaster's people inna dis plantation but more will come for true from all over dis land and across de blue waters."

Everyone volunteered, Keverton and I included. Tacky was visibly moved at the display of intent. He didn't choose Keverton or me but sent two older men ahead to check the road. We watched them disappear into blackness along the winding track.

Tacky then led us back to the wheelhouse. When we arrived, he said, "Me waiting for somebody."

"Waiting for who?" Old Misser Cliff asked.

"Somebody many of you nuh see for ah long time," Tacky said. "When him reach we will mek we move."

"Who is dis somebody?" I whispered in Keverton's ear.

"Me nuh know," Keverton replied, though he smiled a knowing smile.

Chickens were plucked and made ready for roasting in the next half hour. Jars and urns were filled from the river. Scallion Mon, Keverton, myself, and a few others offered more prayers to Bele Alua. Excited chatter of freedom bounced from lip to ear and filled our hopes and dreams. Unaware of their fate, the goats bleated happily enough. Throughout this time, Tacky stood still outside the wheelhouse. He peered into the bush with unblinking eyes like he was waiting for an Akan god.

Finally, someone emerged. His feet were the same tint as the undergrowth. His pants were a similar hue as the tree bark and his limbs were even thicker than Tacky's. Untamed hair crowned his determined forehead. His eyes were quick and alert. You could have hammered in a long post with his mighty jawbone. Slavemasters would have paid a hundred pounds for him. For a short moment, I wondered if I was looking upon one of Bele Alua's pickney.

Tacky spread his arms wide as his mouth curled

into a smile. He strode toward the man. "Midge-wood!" he hailed. "*Maa ho.*"

"*Maa ho?*" I whispered to Keverton. "What dat mean?"

"Good evening."

The two men embraced, like long-lost brothers. Other men hugged the man, including Keverton. I soon realized that there were many things I didn't know or wasn't aware of. *Maybe becah me too young?*

"So you kill off Misser Master?" Midgewood wanted to know.

"Not before him fire ah musket and kill off Cudgemon," replied Tacky. "But Misser Master beg for mercy before him last breath. Me nuh remember him checking him stroke when him using him back-ripper 'pon we. Not at all. So me nuh hesitate wid me final chop."

Midgewood paused a moment to take in the news. "It shoulda been me who kill him, Tacky."

Tacky nodded. "Yes, him nearly kill you for true. But every mon here had plenty reason to out him light."

"Me prepare ah place for you up inna de hills," Midgewood said. "But before me tek you there me have to say me last words to Cudgemon and sprinkle some good water 'pon him grave. Him ah true Akan warrior. May Nyame tek good care of him."

"Me will tek you there," offered Tacky.

Midgewood turned to Keverton. "Keverton, how is me mama keeping? She still smiling and showing her good teet'?"

"She keeping good," said Keverton. "But she nuh smile too much since Miss Pam drop and gone."

"Miss Pam?"

"Yes," said Tacky. "Me good sister. Healer of de plantation, we called her. De river source of Anancy story. De carrier of we gods' stories . . . It still pain me. Her spirit won't let me catch sleep."

He paused for a moment, then glanced up to the skies as if he were asking Nyame why He forsake his good sister. I almost expected Nyame to answer back but He didn't.

"Come, Midgewood," Tacky said after a while. "Let me tek you to Cudgemon. We'll chant by him graveside to help him journey to we ancestors and we'll remember Miss Pam too."

While Tacky and Midgewood were gone, we refreshed ourselves with coconuts and water. A few men, Scallion Mon included, sat in silence and prayed.

It was a good feeling that we could eat, drink, and relax at a time of our own choosing. The other men swapped tales of petrified slavemasters and grisly descriptions of their death poses. Inside my head, I couldn't escape Misser Donaldson's dead body. I wanted to talk to Keverton about it but not with so many of my brothers around. I didn't want to appear weak-hearted.

Midgewood and Tacky returned after a short while and led us into the hills. It was a strange feeling trodding to a place that was forbidden to me before. I kept checking over my shoulder to see if slavemasters were chasing us. My nerves wouldn't stop pinching my heart.

At times during our ascent we hurdled over deep gashes in the earth, crossed crumbling gullies, and scaled steep ridges. It was utterly dark but Midgewood seemed to know where he was heading. The goats found a surer footing than we did. The squawks and tweets sounded stranger the higher we climbed. The mosquitoes buzzed louder and seemed fatter. They were definitely hungrier. I didn't recognize the oddly shaped green creatures with long tails that scurried up the tree trunks. My leg muscles screamed but I didn't complain. I wanted my brothers to know that I was as strong as them, but truth be told, my lungs disagreed with my good foot. I wanted the light to come quick-time so I could view the world from this new place.

10

SOURSOP, GUINEP, AND ROAST CHICKEN

We finally arrived at a clearing. Old Misser Cliff struck and rubbed two pieces of deadwood together and started a small fire. From its light, I noticed strange fruits and shapes lying on the ground. The goats were tied to tree trunks and they nibbled what grass they could find.

Tacky smiled. "You have been well busy," he said to Midgewood.

"Yes, mon," smiled Midgewood. "Me have water coconut, mango, June plum, sweetsop, soursop, and guava."

We didn't need a second invitation. We dined on the fruit as Midgewood and Tacky roasted chickens on a spit fire. I particularly enjoyed the sweetsop. I had never tasted it before. It had a lumpy green skin but its white flesh was delicious and creamy. I chased it down with the juice of the water coconut. The roasted chicken pleased my belly well and I didn't have to suck the marrow out of the bones for extra filling like I usually did. I had guinep and soursop afterward. Everyone agreed it was the best meal we ever had. *No slavemaster to order me back to work.* For the first time in my life, my stomach was full. It was a weird feeling. I usually stood up following a meal, but on this night my body felt heavy.

"Eat good," Tacky said. "De battle nuh finish yet so you will need all de strength to fill up you body you cyan find. Remember, freedom will strike de Trinity plantation before de sun tek her morning yawn."

"De moon is still high so we have time for ah liccle rest," said Louis.

"You have time," Tacky said, "but no rest for Midgewood and meself. We'll tek food down to de men who ah watch de road and then me have to tek Midgewood to see him mama, Miss Gloria. If me don't, me sure Miss Gloria will truly hunt me down and out me light. Then we have to move Miss Pam body and bury her outside de plantation. She deserve to tek her rest beside long tree and hear de rush of de talking skinny river."

"Cyan we help you wid dat?" offered Scallion Mon.

"You nuh want me to chant for Miss Pam again?" asked Old Misser Cliff.

"No, mon," Tacky replied. "It's someting Midgewood and me have to do by weselves."

Midgewood wrapped the fruits and chicken slices in broad leaves and then set off with Tacky. As they vanished into the bush, I turned to Keverton. He feasted on June plum and licked his fingers. Chicken bones were about his feet.

"How . . . how many white mon at dis Trinity plantation?" I asked.

Keverton shook his head and continued eating.

I turned to Louis. "How many?"

"Only Midgewood know," Louis said. "When him come back him cyan tell you. Right about now, you have to catch you sleep."

"But me cyan't sleep if me nuh know how many slavemaster me have to kill," I said.

"Whether it is one or ah hunnerd," Old Misser Cliff said, "do you t'ink you cyan kill any if you nuh catch you rest?"

Keverton nodded. I made a space for myself and stretched out my weary body on the firm ground. I inspected my fingernails and found I still had Misser Donaldson's dried blood wedged behind them. A sudden chill surged through my spine. *Me tek de life of ah white mon. No chicken will slip down him throat again, no mad cane water will touch him lips, and no hand will grip him back-ripper.*

I'm not sure how long I slept but I was awoken by the tooting of a Patoo. Scallion Mon once told me that the promise of death was close by if you see *dem bird wid de long look.* Its big brown eyes stared at me, and sweat covered my brow.

Somehow it felt warmer and more humid high up in the bush than it did in my hut. Keverton and the other men dozed around me. It was dark but the stars I could see through the canopy seemed to shine as brightly as I'd ever seen them. The embers of the fire glowed orange. It spat and crackled every now and then. The aroma of roast chicken lingered in the air, and I could still taste the sweetsop on my tongue. Again, I wanted the sun to bless the morning so I could see this new world.

Two men were in quiet conversation around the ashes—Tacky and Midgewood. I got up and joined them. Their hands were stained with mud.

Midgewood offered me a mango. Only my mama ever gave me fruit before. Tacky placed a hand on my shoulder and set his gaze on me. He had kind but troubled eyes. Again, my heart punched fast and hard. "You sleep good, Moa?"

I nodded.

"Keverton tell me you tek de light outta Misser Donaldson," Tacky said.

"Ah true," I replied.

"An evil mon," Tacky said. "Him reap what him sow. De John Crow will nibble him bones."

I bit a generous piece of my mango and it tasted so good. The juice ran over my chin. I licked my lips.

"Me have ah message from you papa," Tacky revealed. He exchanged a cautious glance with Midgewood before he continued. "He was up by de big house to see what going on. Me promised him me would tek him words to you."

"What . . . what him say?"

"Him say you can still go back," Tacky told me. "And nobody would stop you if you decided to return. You done your part. You de youngest here so. Me have to tek dat into consideration. De battle will be hotter from now on."

"Me might be de youngest but Misser Donaldson use him back-ripper 'pon me de same way like him use it 'pon Keverton. Him never cared about me fourteen years. And me nuh t'ink dat Keverton would like me to leave him. Me like ah true-true brudder to him. No, mon. Me stay here so."

Tacky peered into the ashes and thought about something. I guessed something dark and foreboding menaced his mind. Maybe sadness still licked his heart after reburying Miss Pam.

I had to wait until he had eaten a mango before he spoke again. "Me cyan't promise freedom or life for nobody," he said. "And you know dat for true becah you bury de mighty Cudgemon. At least slavemaster cyan't no more pay one hundred and fifty pounds for Cudgemon."

"Him worth more than dat," Midgewood said. "To we people."

Tacky nodded. "Bless Cudgemon mighty spirit. And me cyan promise dat any brudder who follow me will die for someting. Yes, mon. Better to die for someting than dead becah you body mash up in service to de slavemaster. But remember, Moa, you nuh reach you full size yet. You papa remind me of dat."

I searched Tacky's eyes and allowed his words to linger in my ears. "But . . ." I started. "But nobody cyan promise me life at de plantation. Not even me papa."

"You de last bwoy-chile of you papa," Tacky said. "Him nuh want you to dead before him. Him nuh want to dig you pit. No papa should have to do dat. After him see me and pass me him message, him walk back to him cabin. He has chosen. Him will dead in him cabin or de millhouse."

"Nobody cyan choose when dem dead," I said.

"Ah true ting dat," said Midgewood.

"So you want to give me you good foot and hand for de fight at de Trinity plantation?" Tacky asked. "As me said, it'll only get hotter. Slavemaster people get vex when somebody put dem money inna big danger."

I didn't hesitate. "Yes, mon! Me give you me two hand and me two foot. No turning back now."

Tacky grinned and slapped me hard on the shoulder.

"What is ever'body doing back there ah plantation?" I asked.

"Some of de women are cooking big dinner," he said. "Some are teking dem rest. Some are repairing garment. Me sight ah old mon drinking de firewater."

Midgewood laughed. "Him drink it too fast and burn up him tongue and fry him throat."

"De pickney running about like dem never run about before," smiled Tacky. "Some are praying to we gods."

"De mon?" I asked. "What dem doing?"

"We put some mon on guard," replied Midgewood. "We have eyes watching down by de front gate and every other corner."

"So dem safe for now?" I said.

"For now," replied Tacky. "When war over me will move ever'body to ah nice place. We Dreamland."

"Big war will come," said Midgewood. "But we gods will mek we hands strong and mighty to fight dem."

Dread and the hope of our Dreamland churned in my belly.

11

THE TRINITY PLANTATION

Nobody spoke much as we prepared to leave. Staring at the heavens with his hands above his head, Scallion Mon prayed.

Mooker came over to me. He didn't say anything. He simply looked into my eyes and smacked my shoulder in encouragement. In all my days I had never heard him utter a single word—I wondered if Misser Berris had pulled out his tongue.

After everyone had eaten, Tacky ordered us to sit in a circle. He stood up in the middle and slowly paced back and forward. Again, he studied the gaze of every man. I guessed he judged our hearts too. Meanwhile, Midgewood dropped earth and grass over the dying fire. Dark smoke coiled through the canopy. We all gripped our knives and weapons. I didn't admit it to anyone but I wanted to stay up in the hills for un-told moons feasting on chicken, goats, sweetsop, and water coconuts.

"You done so good, me mighty cane warriors," Tacky started. "But if me know anyting about de slavemasters, dem will send in more to fight we. You body strong like de broad mahoe trees. We must free we Akan brudders and sisters at de Trinity plantation. Nobody free till ever'body free."

"How many slavemaster people there so?" Corn-mon asked.

"About de same amount as de Frontier planta-tion," Midgewood said. "De master there have ah musket too. And him ways are ugly, terrible, and bru-tal. If anybody try and run away, he will chop off de foot and stop de red flow of life wid fire."

My brothers glanced at one another. I looked at my right foot, twitched it, and couldn't imagine los-ing it.

"So Louis, Midgewood, and meself will start de revolution at de master big house," Tacky said. "We will kill everyone in there while dem sleeping."

"Including de pickney?" Scallion Mon asked.

Silence once more.

"If . . . if we find dem," Tacky said. "Then . . . yes."

"Asase Ya and Bele Alua nuh punish we yet," Louis raised his voice. "Dem looking after we."

Mooker and many of the others nodded. "*Awwurra!*"

I swapped glances with Keverton. I had slain a man already but that victory couldn't stop the grinding sensation in my stomach, the rapid beat of my heart, and the sweat dripping off my nosebridge. I wasn't sure if I could do it again.

"After we kill off de slavemaster at Trinity, then we forward march to Fort Haldane," Tacky went on.

"*Awwurra!*" men hollered.

I joined in: "*Awwurra!*"

The chanting blended into excited chatter.

"How far is dis Fort Haldane?" I asked Keverton. "Me foot well tired."

"Midgewood say it's high up by de blue waters," Keverton replied. "Dem have ah whole heap of musket there so."

"Muskets?"

"Yes, Moa. We have to tek de fort to get de muskets. Plenty white mon there so."

I imagined my own burial where my gunshot-riddled body was lowered into a pit just like Cudgemon's. I hoped Old Misser Cliff would chant a lament for me. The Akan gods had truly blessed his voice.

"When de last battle is over," Tacky resumed, "we will find ah good place to live where we cyan raise we own goats, hogs, and chickens, and plant we own fruits and vegetables. It'll be ah nice place where no-body walks wid ah back-ripper and everyone smiling when dem get up in de morning. It'll be ah place where we women nuh have to go to any slavemaster cabin ah nighttime. It'll be ah place where we pick-ney cyan play tee-tah-toe in de afternoon. It'll be ah place where in de quiet, still evening time, we'll sing we songs to Nyame, Asase Ya, and Bele Alua. It'll be we Dreamland."

I closed my eyes and tried to picture such a thing. *Yes, me would tek Mama, Hopie, Hamaya, and even Papa to live there.*

I opened my eyes just as Tacky raised his billhook above his head. "But before we find ah good place, we have to kill off de slavemaster and all who follow him. We cyan't leave any of dem alive."

"Awwurra!" the men chanted. *"Awwurra!"* Unimpressed, the goats continued to feed on the grass.

Midgewood led the way. I'll never know how he navigated a course in the absolute dark. I guessed we kept to high ground but I wasn't too sure. On occasion Midgewood and Tacky had to employ their billhooks to thrash out a path. Birds squawked and flapped above when they did so. At times the undergrowth clawed and scored my skin. There was no breeze to refresh my cheeks or cool my forehead. We passed through a palmetto grove, the leaves patterned like a green fan. Trekking through a fern gully, I noticed how pretty the leaves were. It was like someone had stopped by and decided to snip and shear the foliage for their own pleasure.

It was exciting to trod my good foot in new lands. But fear walked in the back of my head. My heart drummed twice for every step. I expected to see Misser Donaldson around every twist and turn. *Is dis ah dream or are we really trodding freely inna de hills?*

My leg muscles burned as I tried to keep my pace up behind Keverton. Now and again, he glanced over his shoulder and asked, "You all right, Moa?"

"Me foot strong, mon. And me courage fat. Nuh worry about me."

We stopped once for a coconut water break but Midgewood maintained an unrelenting march.

Finally, Tacky raised a hand. We were told to keep quiet and be still as Tacky and Midgewood scouted ahead. Total night hugged us tight. Water coconuts were shared.

Dread crept into my veins and my heartbeat raced like a hunted runaway slave. *All de overseers dem might have muskets.* Part of me wanted to go back to the clearing and dine on more chicken. But there I was, trying to prepare my mind to kill again. Misser Donaldson's lifeless body grew large in my mind. His pale skin. His empty eyes. His lips pressed against the dusty floor. His dried blood discoloring my fingernails. It was proving impossible to rid myself of it.

Moments later, Tacky returned. He spoke in a near whisper. "De Trinity plantation is below we," he said. "De slavemaster's big house is not too far. Now, follow me but keep you foot and mout' silent. Don't even mek ah noise wid you breath."

We slinked through the trees as quiet as shadows until we emerged out of the high woods. The terrain before us fell away sharply. Wild grass climbed above our knees. The talkative cicadas never rested. Somewhere in the distance, I heard the trickle of a skinny river. Thirst scratched the back of my throat. Fire torches ringed the big house. Smoke discharged from two outhouses behind the mansion. I recalled Mama telling me that she and her sisters had to rise before the sun to start the fires in the kitchens. I wondered if the women and girls who worked there were similar to Mama and Hamaya. If Hopie survived childhood, she'd be expected to follow their fate. They would come for her when she reached her size. My blood started to bubble inside of me.

Cabins and huts lined either side of a dirt track that zigzagged downhill from the front lawns. It was almost identical to our home plantation. Tacky raised his arm again. He signaled us to lie close to the ground.

"De overseer live inna de huts close to de big house," Tacky whispered. "Five huts either side of de track where dem live."

"How many live in each hut?" Cornmon asked quietly. His top garment was stained in perspiration and sweat dripped from his forehead.

"Sometime one," Midgewood replied. "Sometime two. Me nuh too sure."

Tacky turned to the rest of us. "When you see de big house catch ah fire, you know de master dead. Dat is you signal."

"Awwurra!"

"Rest you tongue, Scallion Mon," warned Tacky. "Even de green lizard must not hear we."

"Some of we Akan brudders know we coming," said Midgewood in a hush.

"Kill every white mon you see," ordered Tacky. "We cyan't afford any to escape becah dem will ring de alarm. Plenty mon will come in dem big boats into Port Maria hunting for we."

"More?" someone said behind me. "Where do dem come from? Dem breed inna de sea?"

"No, mon," Scallion Mon said. "Dem lived on de moon. Dem even bruise its surface. Nyame did nuh like dem there so He mek dem tumble down to de seas . . . but dem survive. It's why dem prefer big boats to good green lands."

No one questioned Scallion Mon's version of white man history.

Tacky, Midgewood, and Louis punched our shoulders before they sidestepped carefully down a sheer ridge. Their billhooks were drawn.

The deep night soon camouflaged their figures. The fire lamps danced and flickered in the valley below, while the sky still had its full complement of stars. I turned to Keverton and whispered to him, "Say . . . say we nuh see de big house catch ah fire? What do we do then?"

"We go back to de clearing where de goats dem ah nibble," replied Keverton.

"But Midgewood gone wid Tacky," I raised my voice. "Nobody else know de way."

"Moa, hush you mout'!" rebuked Old Misser Cliff. "You have more questions than ah field of crickets. Do you want de slavemaster to hear you?"

The next few minutes were the longest in my life. I couldn't see the insects around me but they screeched and squealed into my ears. I wanted to stamp on all of them. Impatience twitched my toes and flicked my eyes. I wasn't the only one to fidget and breathe heavy while waiting.

A gunshot cut the Jamaican night. Then another.

I lifted my head but couldn't see what was taking place. Curses and shouts came from the big house.

Still no fire. The men around me leaped to their feet. Heat flooded my veins and made them fat. Mooker was the first to break into a sprint. Pure rage was in his eyes as he pinned his head back, held his billhook ahead of him, and careered down the hill.

"Hold on! Hold on!" Old Misser Cliff cried.

Mooker kept on running before he disappeared into the night.

Then, far down below, a spark of flame. It blazed out of one of the front windows from the big house. I could make out the shape of the front lawn. Before my feet overcame my anxiety, Old Misser Cliff, Scallion Mon, and Cornmon had already sprung forward and charged toward the overseer huts.

"Asase Ya!"

"Bele Alua!"

Everyone followed.

"Come, Moa!" roared Keverton. He brandished his billhook above his head.

Thick tussocky grass grew in bunches down the hill and I had to dodge mud clumps and divots. It was treacherous. Twice I tripped over. On the second occasion I dropped my blade.

"Moa, tek time," Keverton said as I fumbled for it. "Remember, if you lose you knife, you could lose you life."

Ignoring Keverton, I now ran at full speed. The

land leveled as we neared the big house. I jumped over a log fence. Shrieks and cries surrounded us. One outhouse was already ablaze. Slaves poured out of their huts behind the big house. Some gripped cutlasses and billhooks. Others clutched bedposts, rakes, hoes, forks, wheel spokes, and any other sharp or solid implement they could find.

I found myself close to the front of the mansion. Flames licked out of one of the first-floor windows— smoke filled my nostrils. The dirt road sloped down to my left. It was then that I spotted five overseers. One of them rushed toward me. He wore white pants and was bare-chested. His feet were naked. A thick beard hid his lips. In his left hand he grasped a long curved blade that glinted under the moonlight. Its cutting edge promised death. For a moment I froze to the spot and thought of the Patoo owl. The only moving part of my body was my rapid-beating heart. My brain commanded me to flee or fight but my limbs wouldn't respond.

Twenty strides away. My feet seemed chained to the ground.

Ten strides away. He yelled something at me. His cheeks were blistered, peeling, and red. His eyes spoke of disgust.

Five strides away. Suddenly Keverton appeared out of nowhere and cut the man down. He hacked the overseer just above his right knee. The white man howled in agony. Without further ado, Keverton carved his throat as skillfully as he cut the cane. No more sound came from the man's mouth. He dropped to the ground as dead as a stalk flung into Hamaya's handcart.

"Moa!" Keverton cried.

I turned around. Another man raced toward me. He swished and swashed his sword as if he was at war with an army of mosquitoes. He bared his broken teeth. He cried a strange cry. His tongue was more brown than pink and his breath reeked of tobacco. No time to think. Finally my feet obeyed my orders. I dropped to the ground and targeted his calves. I felt the wind of his thrusts but my aim was powerful and true. I caught him just behind his right knee and then stabbed him in the groin. I didn't give him another opportunity to decapitate me. Within seconds he would never be able to swallow. Not even a crumb. I stood over his body, but this time I didn't meet his eyes. Instead, I watched his blood drain from his neck and form an oval pool on the ground.

My eyes darted here and there to check what occurred about me. Three women had clubbed a short white man senseless with a fence post. One slave repeatedly flogged an already dead overseer. Other white men screamed their agonies. One begged for his Jesus to save him.

A single cockerel announced the coming of dawn.

My brothers and sisters rejoiced, danced, and chanted prayers to Nyame, Asase Ya, and Bele Alua.

Then I heard Tacky's voice: "Nuh let any of dem escape!"

Before I could check where Tacky was, I felt a strong hand pressed on my back. I gripped my billhook hard and raised it high. Before I brought it down in a chopping motion, I recognized Keverton. My mouth released my longest-ever breath.

"Moa!" he yelled. "You want to kill me?"

"No, mon, me t'ought you was—"

"One of dem run to de bush," Keverton cut me off. "Come, mon."

We sprinted into some nearby woods where many of the young trees were stunted or hacked down— Bele Alua would surely take Her revenge. No star or firelight penetrated, so Keverton and I kept close together. We ran into a deep hollow. For half an hour or so, we frantically searched high and low and broad and long. Finally, Keverton shook his head. "Him gone," he said. "And me nuh know which way him gone. We better go back and tell Tacky."

By the time we emerged out of the woods, the big house was engulfed in flames. The fingertips of the fire kissed the heavens. I'm sure that even Nyame, our sky god, felt the roasting in His left eye. Brothers and sisters slowly backed away from the mansion in stunned silence. Their eyes were wide and their mouths open. It was a surreal sight, a beautiful dancing orange and yellow.

"Ah shame we burn it down before me could look inside," said Keverton. "Me never plant me good foot inside ah master's big house."

"You nuh want to step inside ah wicked place like dat," I replied.

"Me wanted to sight de bed de master sleep in," said Keverton. "And put me good foot 'pon de staircase. And sit at him long table."

"Dat would have been an experience," I said. "Me still nuh know what it would be like to plant me tired toe 'pon ah second floor of ah big house."

Tacky and Midgewood appeared from the side of the big house. Their faces were smeared with dust, grime, and blood. Louis was with them. His left arm was bandaged in a brown rag, dried blood painted his elbow, and bruises blotched his face. He carried a short musket and, judging by his fierce expression, he wanted to use it quick-time.

"Nuh stand up there so and look 'pon de fire like it put you inna spell!" Tacky shouted. "Only nineteen slavemaster dead. Where de rest of dem?"

"De one we chase, him foot might be bad but it rapid," said Keverton. "Moa and meself look under dis and over dat but no sight of him."

Tacky shook his head.

We checked every cabin, every pit toilet, and every outhouse and shed. I returned to the front lawn wondering if I'd be sent farther afield to hunt down the runaway slavemasters. Exhaustion captured my feet first and rapidly spread throughout the rest of my body. I dropped to the ground. My eyes were about to close when I heard Tacky's voice again. Raw strength, or maybe it was our goddess Abowie's breath, lifted me up once more.

"Me brudders tell me dat there were at least twenty-five overseer here so," Tacky said.

Midgewood stood beside him. "Dem coulda run to de next plantation," he said. "Or dem coulda tek dem bad foot to Fort Haldane."

"How far is de next plantation?" Scallion Mon asked.

"If you have good foot, about ah one-hour trod t'rough de bush."

"So let we march to de next plantation," Old Misser Cliff said. He still held his billhook within his left hand. "Let we kill off all de slavemaster people there so and free we brudders and sisters."

"*Awwurra!*" chanted the freedom fighters. "*Awwurra!*"

"Before we tek up we tired toe and march to de next plantation or anywhere else," Tacky said, "you must rest youself for ah liccle while and eat good. Strong body we need."

"And then we forward to de next plantation after dat?" Old Misser Cliff wanted to know.

Tacky shook his head. He thought about something. "No, mon. We have to capture de fort first and kill de mon there so. It will cause ah whole heap of confusion for dem. Dat's where de mon in good garments wid same-color hats rest dem head. Dat's where dem mek dem plan. We must scatter dem plans."

"Dem have plenty mon there wid nuff musket," said Midgewood. "Better we kill dem before somebody tell dem about we."

"After we capture de fort," Tacky explained, "some of we cyan march to de next plantation."

"But nuh worry about dat now," said Louis. "Let's find some good food and eat."

Keverton's grin was as wide as a soursop.

Women and girls smiled and hugged us before they raided the slavemaster's kitchen storehouse for bacon, ham, chicken, and vegetables. One of them led Keverton and I back to her cabin. Her name was Nimalpha. She wore a black tie-head and a field-stained dress that tickled her naked toes. Thick black weals covered her neck and left cheek. Her left eye was bloodshot and I didn't want to imagine in what way the slavemaster's evil had disfigured her. Her hands

were as big as mine. I didn't recognize many of her
words.

Nimalpha's hut had four beds fighting for space on
the floor. Lying on one cot was a girl who I guessed
was the same age as me. Her eyes were pretty and
alert. Moonlight shone off her cheeks. She had generous lips, and I liked the shine of her dark skin. A
crutch carved out of a branch lay beside her bed. Her
left leg had been sawed off just below her calf. It had
been dressed in soiled rags. I couldn't help but wince.

She smiled at me. "*Maa ho,*" she said.

"*Maa ho,*" I replied.

She spoke again. I thought she tried to tell me her
name. Malinora, I think she said. I seated myself next
to her and she pulled herself up. She reached out a
hand and caressed my jaw. Her fingers were warm and
tender. She drew a circle on my forehead. There was
no self-pity in her eyes, just a quiet contentment that
I had chosen to sit beside her. Only my mother had
ever touched me like that. It moved me beyond words,
and I had to fight back my tears.

"*Wo ho te sen?*" she said.

I guessed she asked me how I was.

It took me a few moments to remember an Akan
reply. "*Me ho ye.*" My body was fine.

Wooden bowls and mugs rested on a wonky
wooden table in the middle of the room. Moonlight

stole in from the open window. Insects quarreled outside. The stench of a thousand floggings and a million tears seemed to rise from the floorboards. Some small creature I couldn't name scratched somewhere below. Nimalpha shared out the food with a wooden ladle. "Eat quick-time," she said.

I wasn't that hungry but Keverton downed everything offered to him. I couldn't remember ever eating ham and I found it delicious. Nimalpha was happy to offer me more.

"We catch victory here so," Keverton said. "But we nuh know when we cyan eat good like dis again so we must enjoy dis blessing."

Moments later, Louis called us out.

I took one last look at the girl with one foot, raised my fist, and chanted, *"Awwurra!"*

"Awwurra!" Keverton and the girls repeated. "De blood remembers."

I wanted to stay but we had to go. I had never thought of being with a woman before, but the girl with one foot would occupy my thoughts and dreams for the longest time.

We made our way back to the lawn in front of the big house. The fire still raged. Walls blackened, split, and crumbled. Roofs disintegrated and crashed down. Specks of hot dust and ash found a way to my lungs. I coughed and spluttered before I backed off a few strides. Rebels watched with unblinking eyes. I wondered if they shared my thoughts. *Dis really happening. Dem will kill we for true for dis. Dem will starve we in cages. Dem will rip off we manhood. Dem will rape we women in plain sight of we. Many ah pit will be dug. Small pickney will be forced to watch.*

I drained the juice of a water coconut before Tacky stood up and examined our eyes again. "Get youself inna circle," he ordered. We did what we were told. Tacky was impressed by how quickly we moved. Truth be told, I wanted to lie back down. "Ever'body ready?" he asked.

"Awwurra!"

"To Fort Haldane! If any slavemaster come in we way, let dem blood drip de rusty side of me billhook!"

"Awwurra!"

Before we set off, Tacky slowly approached me. He looked at me hard and whispered into my ear, "You done good, Moa. Me well proud of you. But you cyan't count as many moons as de rest of we. If you want to, you cyan stay here so and help mind de woman and pickney. De slavemasters who tek dem bad foot to de bush might come back."

For a short moment I thought of Nimalpha and the girl who only had five toes. But I had killed two men. I wouldn't hesitate again. *Dem will need me to slay more.*

I gazed at my right hand and wondered how many more lives it would take. "No, mon," I replied. "Me cyan't do dat. Me nuh want to leave Keverton side. Him need me and me need him."

"All right," Tacky said. "Strong you are strong. And you and Keverton mek ah devastating combination."

We picked up our weapons and marched down the dirt track. Someone sang an Akan song. Old Misser Cliff and Scallion Mon looked up to the skies. Freedom fighters who recognized the tune hummed along and I tried to chant with them to sound as one. Determination swelled inside me. Women and young pickney emerged out of their cabins and watched us on our way. They said farewell. Some of them wept but others smiled. One or two didn't quite know what to make of it all, like they were frightened to believe what had just occurred or didn't want to invite bad fortune by expressing joy.

My heart bruised my chest for I knew I was trodding into danger once again. I thought of Papa sitting in his millhouse. *You see, Papa, no matter what happens now, me mek me contribution. No mon cyan dispute dat. Me might not ah grow to me full size yet but me's ah mon now.*

I recalled Tacky's words: *Better to die for someting than dead becah you body mash up in service to de slavemaster.*

I looked out for Nimalpha and the girl with one foot. I didn't know at the time that I'd never see her again. Her kind, half moon–shaped eyes would stay with me until my end.

12

FORT HALDANE

After Scallion Mon chanted a prayer to the healing goddess Abowie, seventy men trod their good foot to Fort Haldane that early morning. Twenty of our older and younger brothers stayed behind to defend the women and pickney. Tacky and Midgewood led the way. Louis proudly held his musket close to his chest. The rest of us carried water urns and water coconuts. An uncountable number of unseen roosters proclaimed the spreading dawn. The green of the land started to exert itself as the sun blessed the high peaks of the eastern ranges. I'd never appreciated it before but the land was a rich green and well pretty. It felt strange to plant my good foot on fresh turf. Maybe I saw it that way because I couldn't see any well-trodden pathways that lined the plantation. I still peered around bush corners and into deep gullies, expecting slavemasters to attack us.

The dirt track widened the farther we stepped. The carriage wheel ruts were a forefinger deep and two cane stalks wide. It seemed that every hill that we crested, another one was waiting for us. We only stopped once for a water break before Midgewood set off again. His calf muscles were round and hard and his thighs challenged the tree trunks. Old Misser Cliff renamed him *Longstride*.

Finally, Midgewood raised an arm. He stood very still at the peak of yet another rise and looked straight ahead. Tacky joined him before the rest of us caught up with them. We came off the dirt track and stood abreast upon the summit. At first, I only saw a blue haze. Then my eyes adjusted to the light and I could make out the wide blue waters. They went on forever until they kissed the horizon. I marveled at the sight. Something strange happened in my chest, as if my blood recalled the loss of our ancestors. I found it hard to believe that my fathers and mothers before me had crossed such a vast expanse of sea. It didn't seem possible.

"Dat is ah pretty sight for ah weary eye, me ah tell you," Keverton said.

"Ah true ting you ah say," I replied.

"No wide blue waters will wet we good skin to-day," Tacky said. "And even though it look well nice, remember dat too many of we brudders and sisters were flung into de deep when sickness catch dem. Nyame, Asase Ya, and Bele Alua have to dip inna de sea to find de spirits of we people."

"Me never know dat," said Keverton.

"And now you do know," said Tacky. "Pass it on to you pickney if you ever blessed wid dem. Now look to you lef'."

Everyone gazed westward but none of us were sure what we were looking at. Midgewood pointed at a hill overlooking the ocean. "Fort Haldane is up there so," he said. "Ah building made of stone heavy like hog belly. Dem have two mighty guns pointing out to de broad waters. Me never see dem fire dem, but if dem do, dem must sure mash up de big boats and send dem to kiss de sea bottom."

"How big are these guns?" I wanted to know.

"Dem as long as two good piece of cane join together," replied Midgewood. "And round and big like Cornmon head."

"Ah good ting dem not pointing at we," Old Misser Cliff said.

I squinted and could just make out a gray rectangular structure. I guessed it was another hour's trod away. "How . . . how many slavemaster people up there so?"

"Sometime four," Midgewood responded. "Sometime me sight six of dem. It's hard to guess becah most of de time dem inside. And dem nuh have any front or back window. De front door always close. Sometime me spy 'pon dem when dem outside. Dem drink firewater, do dem funny dance, and sing dem strange song. Sometime dem bring we women there."

"Why never five of dem in there?" Keverton asked.

"Maybe sometime five too," Midgewood said. "Me cyan't tell. Dem come and go."

"No problem," said Cornmon. "Didn't we just kill off nineteen white mon at de Trinity plantation?"

"Yes, we did," said Tacky. "But the four, five, or six mon at Fort Haldane have ah wagonload of muskets. And it's where dem keep dem gunpowder too. And nuh forget dat de white mon who escape from Trinity might be there so too."

"You t'ink dem foot dat fast?" I asked.

"If none of dem have touched de firewater last night before we come, then it's possible," Tacky replied. "Remember, dem start trod when de sun was sleeping."

"So how do we attack ah place like dat?" Old Misser Cliff asked.

Tacky smiled and thought about it. "We just have to be patient and careful in we approach. From here so, we trod in single file. All of we walk ten strides from each other. When we get close, we hide behind any tree or bush we cyan find. Bele Alua will protect we. Me want to lick dem wid surprise like heavy coconut dropping 'pon ah bwoy-chile wid ah skinny head."

"There is no tree broad enough for Cornmon," said Old Misser Cliff. "Maybe he cyan carry ah wide bush 'pon him back and hide behind dat when him need to. Fat him fat."

Everyone looked at Cornmon, who owned a generous stomach, and burst into laughter. It felt good to grin about something. Cornmon took it well but Old Misser Cliff was right—Cornmon was hard to hide.

My heart kept up its beating against my ribs.

"Cornmon cyan tek up de rear," Tacky decided. "It's an important position becah we need strong eyes to check what's behind we."

"What happen when we get there?" Keverton asked.

"We wait," said Tacky. "Midgewood tell me dat de pit toilet is about ten strides away from de guns. Sooner or later every mon have to use it. Dat is where we will lick dem down."

Louis held his musket aloft. He waved it this way and that with his finger brushing the trigger. "Me get me chance to use me musket? Let dem taste quick deat'. Let me shoot one of dem like Misser Master shot Cudgemon—may de Akan gods tek him spirit."

"If you keep playing wid dat musket you might

shoot all of we," said Old Misser Cliff. "Me nuh tek part in dis uprising just to get shoot up by me own blood. Aim you musket to de ground so if you fire by mistake we only lose you broad toes and get lick by flying toenail."

Tacky laughed, then shook his head. "No, Louis. Only use de musket as ah last resort. Let sharp steel, tough wood, and hard knuckle do its work."

"We nuh really know how many white mon around who might hear gunshot," said Midgewood. "Remember, six of dem escape from Trinity."

"Ever'body tek you last drink now," ordered Tacky. "Then leave you water here so. Me want you hands to be free."

Everyone did what we were told. We gazed ahead and awaited Tacky's signal. It was a quiet moment and I thought of Papa and his lost arm. *Me shoulda burn down de millhouse to force him to come wid we. But even if he did tek him good foot to join we, he'd always be at ah disadvantage.* I found myself squeezing the handle of my billhook.

"Ten strides apart," Tacky told us. "Try and keep behind tree when you have de chance."

Swerving hills, open fields, and untamed grass lay ahead of us. Only a wide thin arch of the distant western sky hadn't been touched by the rising sun. Louis took the lead, his musket poised in front of him. Tacky was next, followed by Midgewood. Led by the tones of Scallion Mon, we hummed another Akan spiritual. I felt blisters forming on my soles and my neck was stinging fierce where Misser Donaldson's lash had ripped into me.

The swell of land that we followed rose steadily as we approached the coast. The air was cleaner. Trees became farther apart. The coarse grass became paler, almost yellow. The broad blue waters were perfectly still. I sensed Keverton's breathing rhythm behind me. I wondered if he felt the same dread flooding through his veins as I did. *Dem have untold musket. We only have one.*

Three hundred strides away.

We halted our march behind a family of jacaranda trees. The smell was pleasant and we were grateful for the shade. I sat down and fanned myself with a broad leaf. I could see the fort clearly now. It was about five cabins wide and two men high. I couldn't tell you what materials they had used to build the structure but it rose ominously out of the ground, harsh and hard. The widest door I had ever seen was set in the front wall. I couldn't see any windows.

Handcarts lay upon a dirt path. I thought of Hamaya and hoped I'd see her defiant face again. *At least she wouldn't have to wheel ah cartload of cane to de millhouse on dis morning. Maybe she teaching liccle Hopie some Akan words.*

A waist-high log fence, with a gate in the middle, encircled the compound. Seven tall coconut trees of almost identical size fronted the fort. From the entrance, a pathway twisted its way through thick bushes, scrub, and trees down to the town of Port Maria about two miles away. Two donkeys tied to ropes nibbled on an apron of grass close to the front door. I couldn't see the chickens but they answered their cousins in the hills behind me. No white man was in sight. I hoped none of them were inside. All seemed as quiet and calm as the bright blue seas rippled gently in the distance.

A nervous storm brewed inside my stomach. Misser Donaldson's corpse appeared in my mind once again.

"There is ah back door," said Midgewood. "And de pit toilet is out back too."

"We'll strike there first," said Tacky. "As me say, every mon have to relieve demself sooner or later."

"Let me lead de way," said Midgewood. "Me know de trees and bush good here so."

"Me should go first," Louis said. "Me have de musket and me know how to use it. Let dem taste quick deat'."

"No, mon," said Tacky. "Let Midgewood plant him foot up de hill. Him know de best way."

Midgewood smiled at all of us before he turned

his attention to the fort. He concentrated his eyes and sniffed the air, then set off two hundred or so strides to the right. He found cover behind a guango tree. My eyes switched to the fort's front door. I expected it to open with a thousand white men rushing out of it at any moment firing their long muskets and swish-swashing their even longer swords.

Midgewood didn't wait too long. Quick-footed like a he-goat charging toward an enemy, he darted to another tree. Tacky took that as a cue for him to dash to the first cover.

Within fifteen minutes, fifty of us crouched behind bushes and a fold of the land to the right of the fort, close to the dirt path. We had positioned ourselves thirty strides away. Tacky had ordered the rest of our company, including Cornmon, to wait at two hilltops inland. A keen breeze drifted in from the ocean. I tasted salt in the air. The clean blue waters lapped and ebbed beneath us as a merciless sun blazed above. A rocky cliff face, clefted with hard earth and deep-rooted plants, dived down to a soft beach. I palmed the sweat from my forehead. The hurricane inside my belly woke again and I felt my last meal rise in my throat.

I could just glimpse the buildings that made up Port Maria along the coast to the east. I imagined there were more enemies down there. There weren't any big boats in port but I spotted the jetties jutting out into the sea like long brown fingers.

From my vantage point I could see the side of the building and the back lawn of the fort. The pale grass was calf-high and the cicadas hadn't concluded their nighttime debate. Housed in what looked like to me a huge handcart were two giant black guns. They targeted the port and the bay below us. Thigh-high wooden barrels sat on the ground beside them—I wondered what was inside them.

A black rooster strutted this way and that in a chicken coop on the far side of the lawn. Seven brown hens watched him. Every time it tested its voice, my nerves exploded. Next to the chicken coop, close to a fence, was a shoulder-high wooden box—the pit toilet. I couldn't lie: I wished I was back with Cornmon even though he couldn't conceal himself well.

"De morning's still young," Tacky said. "But dem will rise soon."

"Sometime ah mon keep ah watch out back at nighttime," said Midgewood. "Dem looking for enemies in big boats. Sometime me hear dem talking. Dem nuh like ah people call *Spanish*."

"Let dem look out to de broad waters and worry about Spanish people," said Tacky. "Terror and deat' coming to dem from inland."

"Why we cyan't just mash down de back door and

kill ever'body inside?" suggested Louis. "There is fifty of we. Let me shoot de first one who step outside and de next one after dat."

"No, mon," replied Tacky. "Remember, you have to reload before you cyan fire two or t'ree shot. Dem have more muskets than we. And dem musket talk quicker than we cyan run."

"What do we do?" I asked.

"Just wait, mon," Tacky said. "And watch de back way. *Never* look forward to war. It'll come to we when it's ready and when it come it never pretty."

I couldn't tell you how long we waited for someone to appear from the back door. It felt like a whole moon cycle. All I could do was grip my billhook tight and pray to Asase Ya that any gunshot and long sharp blade would evade me. *At least if me dead, me cyan say dat me sight de broad blue waters. Me nuh want to tell nobody but me really hope to see ah big boat for de first time.*

The sun had climbed above the eastern hills when we finally heard a sound. A door wailed. Every eye was fixed on the back door. I didn't blink. A tall white man with long hair and a full beard ambled casually to the pit toilet. He yawned and stretched his arms. He peered out to sea. He adjusted a belt around his pants and he sang a strange song. He wasn't as melodic as Old Misser Cliff.

"It seem like him trouble de firewater last night," whispered Midgewood.

Mooker stood up but Tacky pulled him down and beckoned him to wait. The white man opened the door, ducked his head, and went inside. He closed the gate behind him and continued singing. I guessed that Cornmon would have great difficulty fitting inside that wooden box.

Tacky signaled Midgewood and Keverton to skirt the back of the fence and come up behind the pit toilet. Their toes were swift and silent. As they crept into position, the rooster chose this moment to charm the morning once again. His cock-a-doo-a-doo-doo-dooling almost ruptured my good heart and collapsed everything else around it. I had never wanted to kill an animal so much as that damn cockerel.

Midgewood and Keverton crouched at either side of the pit toilet. They stared at each other, knowing that a big moment was before them. The white man stopped warbling. He grunted instead. Then Midgewood readied his billhook and the sun caught its reflection. I opened my mouth. The back of my throat felt dry. I licked my lips. I glanced at my brothers around me and even Tacky appeared anxious. I felt a little jealous that Keverton had been chosen for this mission and I wasn't. At least he was doing something. I could hardly bear to watch. I felt my hard breathing on my hands. My fingers tingled and my feet twitched.

I had never known a man to spend so long taking a shit. *How much waste is inside any mon? Did he eat de horns of ah he-goat?*

Finally, the door creaked. I spotted a white hand pushing the gate open. Without any hesitation Keverton leaped onto the man, covered his mouth with the three fingers on his left hand, and split his throat with his billhook with the other. Midgewood drove and twisted his blade deep into the man's chest. It was over in seconds. The dead man was quickly carried and thrown over the fence. His body tumbled down a steep precipice and landed on hard earth that jutted out of the rock face. It wasn't the end his mama had hoped for.

"*Awwurra!*" Scallion Mon cried. "Bele is wid we!"

Tacky was quick to cover his mouth. "Chant again and me will fling you over de same place where de white mon rest him final rest! Quiet you tongue, Scallion Mon. We wait again."

Tacky signaled for Keverton and Midgewood to hold a position either side of the back door. He indicated the rest of us to climb the fence and lie down flat on the grass. As I took my place behind the pit toilet, I heard the whisper of the ocean and suffered the stench of human waste. I tightly gripped the handle of my billhook. High-pitched-sounding white birds flew over our heads and swooped down to the sea on some business of their own.

This time, we didn't have to wait long.

The back door opened again. Another white man appeared. He had on tight white pants, black boots, and a long blue jacket. He wore a curious expression. Some sort of odd-looking hat crowned his head. "Conway!" he called out. "Where are you? Conway! Are you going to help me clean—"

I couldn't quite tell you how he was killed, but the shock of his gaze at Midgewood's knife will never leave my memory. Mooker and I were ordered to toss the man over the cliff and this time the body bounced off an outcrop of white rock and managed to find itself meeting the soft waves. The white birds investigated the fallen body. I wondered what gods would dive into the blue waters and save the dead man's spirit.

Tacky scurried to meet Keverton and Midgewood by the back door. He gestured for Louis to join him. We readied our knives. I got up to my feet and bent down low. Just as Louis rushed to the back entry, a shot was fired. Everyone ducked.

"Go round to de front!" Tacky cried. "Go round to de front!"

Too late.

Three white men dashed out of the back door

with long muskets. They fired them at will. I saw Old Misser Cliff stagger, fall back, and drop to the ground. His body didn't move. I kept as low as I possibly could but the shots kept coming. One screamed over my head. The noise split my ears. Two more brothers fell.

Louis tried to fire his musket but nothing happened. He threw it away and charged into the fort with only his flailing fists as weapons. Keverton had managed to leap on top of one of the gunmen and grappled with him on the ground, trying to wrest control of the musket, his own blood dripping from his back as his wounds from the back-ripper opened once more.

Another white man in uniform suffered an ugly death: Midgewood gored him through the left ear with his knife. Mooker took one mighty swing of his billhook and instantly killed the white man who had wrestled with Keverton. Blood gushed from the man's nostrils as well as his ear.

"Forward to de front!" Tacky commanded. "Forward to de front! Nuh let any of dem escape!"

For a very short moment, I closed my eyes and willed for Asase Ya to run with me. My blood bubbled behind my forehead.

More than twenty freedom fighters dashed with me around the side of the fort and to the front. The donkeys still nibbled the grass. I spotted one white man racing for his bad life through the line of coconut trees. He looked as young as me. He frantically clambered over the fence. He didn't have a musket. He glanced back once. Sheer fright took up residence in his gaze.

"Awwurra!"

Fresh strength surged through me and I set off in pursuit. Just as I hurdled the front fence, I heard a loud shot. In an instant, a hot pain spread from my shoulder. It seared into me like a branding iron. I lost all feeling in my legs. I landed in a heap on the ground and dizziness seized my eyes. My head felt very heavy. I tried to stand up but my feet and knees failed me. Suddenly the sun burned as hot as the blaze that ripped through the master's big house at Trinity. I collapsed with one arm draped over the first rung of the fence. My head met the ground with a thud. The world spun around me and I couldn't feel the ground.

Memories hot-breezed through my mind. I saw Mama in Misser Master's kitchen lighting the oven fires and preparing the meat to be cooked. I heard little Hopie's first cries just after she was born. I watched Keverton showing me how to cut the sugarcane. Hamaya and her handcart filled another vision. *Dem will soon come for me, Moa.* Finally, Papa was there too, feeding the cane into the wide rollers, his expression grim and defeated. *Better to be living doing dis than dead inna de pit*, he said repeatedly.

Me die for someting, Papa, I said to myself. *Me nuh disgrace me Akan ancestors. Asase Ya will come for me. Me hope dem bury me next to ah good river wid ah mighty tree looking over me. Nuh forget to pour good water over me.*

Giddiness overwhelmed me. I closed my eyes and waited for death.

13

THE WATCHHOUSE

I woke up lying on a bed made of broad fern leaves and straw. *I'm alive!* The room stank of something I wasn't familiar with. I tried to sit up but the throbbing pain from my shoulder stopped me from doing so. My eyes couldn't focus properly. I muttered a quick prayer to Abowie to return my strength.

Blood had stained my shirt and it was torn where I had been shot. Someone had taken off my shoes. The back of my head ached. The soles of my feet were blistered and peeling. My toenails were black and clogged with grit and dry earth. A wooden mug filled with water rested on a bedside cabinet beside me. I struggled through the pain and sat up, then I drank from the mug greedily and splashed a little on my forehead. I blinked the wetness out of my eyes. A small table near the door had a candle and a bible resting upon it—it had the same cross on it that Misser Donaldson's book had on his bedside cabinet. I heard the breath of the sea. The breeze was gentle. Salt was in my nostrils.

I noticed open slits in the thick wall to my right. They were just wide enough to point a long musket through. I peered through one and spotted Keverton sitting down beside the two black guns. He was gazing out to the ocean and chewing and sucking something. I couldn't see the sun so I was unable to guess whether it was morning or afternoon.

"Keverton!" I called. My voice was weak. I tried again: "Keverton!"

He turned around, stood up, and ran to join me. His steps resounded through the fort, and when he stepped through the doorway of my room, his grin was as broad as a fat jackfruit. In his left hand he held a gnawed piece of sugarcane. He wore different boots.

"Moa!" he said. "Abowie and Akonadi give you ah next life! Let me chant dem names!"

"What happen?" I asked. "Where is ever'body? Where you get de boots from?"

"De boots?" Keverton smiled as he admired his new footwear. "From one of de dead white mon. Him nuh need dem no more. Dem fit me good. You nuh t'ink so?"

"What happen?" I repeated.

125

"You get shot by ah long musket," Keverton replied. "Dat's what happen. Eye-water ah drip down me face becah me was wondering how to tell you mama and liccle Hopie. And Hamaya too—she look 'pon you like ah big brudder. But quick deat' nuh knock 'pon you gate yet and me nuh have to dig you deep pit. You chest must be built wid tough-like mahoe tree wood. You survive, Moa! But you better t'ank Asase Ya for Midgewood."

"Midgewood? What did Midgewood do?"

"After de battle," Keverton explained, "we found you near de front fence. You eyes were closed. Some mon t'ought you were on you way to meet we ancestor but Midgewood noticed you were still drawing ah liccle breath. Ah whole heap of you blood wet de ground. Nuff mosquito ah drink it up and fat up dem belly."

"Next time me have chicken me going to give Midgewood all of me slice," I said.

"Yes, mon. And give me two slice and ah fat piece of ham too! But Midgewood save you for true. He run into de bush and find some good leaf. Him boil it up and press it 'pon you wound. It was like Miss Pam come alive in him. Sleep you been sleeping since then. Tacky ask me to stay wid you and mek sure dat de John Crow nuh nibble you."

"Where dem gone?" I asked. "Dem still hunting white mon?"

"Yes, mon. But de battle here so is over. There is ah smaller plantation dat Midgewood did talk about. It's about ah two-hour trod from here so. Tacky want to free slave from there so."

"Another plantation?"

"Yes, Moa," Keverton said. "Only Asase Ya know how many on dis bad place."

"Do we have to kill ah whole heap of more white mon before we find we Dreamland?"

Keverton didn't answer. Instead he looked over my shoulder before he gazed at me again. "Here so, we fling eight white mon over de cliff. Some of dem never reach de sea but de John Crow and de land crabs will get dem belly fat on dem. Some of we brudders get shot in dem leg and arm but dem not too bad and cyan still walk good."

"What about Old Misser Cliff?" I asked. "Me see him drop."

Keverton said nothing. Instead he walked to the oceanside wall and peered through the slits. He sucked on his sugarcane again.

"Old Misser Cliff?" I said again.

Keverton shook his head. "Him try and him try but Midgewood could nuh save him. De gods have called him home. Ever'body's head dropped. Nuff eye-water fall, me ah tell you. Scallion Mon sang him ah pretty song."

In my mind's eye, I saw myself standing in Old Misser Cliff's shed watching him repair Hamaya's handcart. A kind smile twitched his lips. He concentrated his eyes on the broken wheel before him. Maybe he was the only man in our plantation who enjoyed his work. *One good day, de Akan gods will tek dem revenge*, he used to say. *Dem won't let we suffer for too much longer.*

It could have been me. Dis is what Papa warn me about. But at least Old Misser Cliff dead from fighting for freedom.

"Where did dem bury him?" I asked.

"By ah guango tree about ah one mile trod inland," Keverton answered. "We search long time for ah long tree. Him use to love sit down and eat beside another tree like it where Miss Gloria serve her good food. Me help dig de pit and de trench around it. After Scallion Mon start sing, ever'body else chant wid him to help him journey to we ancestor. We pour good water 'pon him."

"When me shoulder good, tek me there," I said. "Me want to chant for Old Misser Cliff too. He was ah good, kind mon."

We shared a quiet moment of sorrow.

I tried to sit up higher, but the pain was too much for me.

"Moa! Keep you good self still there so," said Keverton. "Tacky and Midgewood tell me to mind you. If you try to get up again me will t'ump you down meself."

I lay back down. "What is dis place?"

"It's where de white mon keep dem muskets," Keverton said. "Dem were inna room downstairs."

"Dem have ah downstairs in dis place?" I asked. "Dem live like land crab, blind lizard, and worm?"

"Yes, mon," Keverton replied. "Dem build de place wid tough stone and dem dig deep into de ground. Dem also have ah room wid big maps and charts 'pon ah big table. Tacky and Louis tried to read it but give up. But dem tek dem and found forty muskets down there."

"Forty!"

"Yes, mon. And gunpowder too. Tacky tek it away 'pon ah handcart. Midgewood tek de donkeys too. Me hope Cornmon nuh eat dem. Dem were de fattest donkeys me ever see. De musket dat Louis tek from de master at Trinity had no gunpowder in there so him smiling now."

"Do you have ah musket?"

"Yes, mon, it's in de next room. It's as long as me leg."

"Have you learned how to fire it yet?"

"Louis show me," said Keverton. "Believe me, de first slavemaster who come up here so will suffer ah quick deat'."

"Tacky leave ah long musket for me?"

Keverton shook his head. "Just forty muskets. Not enough for ever'body. Tacky tell me not to waste any gunpowder. And we have ah job to do."

"Ah job?" I repeated. "Me hope nobody ask me to cut de cane again. Me nuh kill two white mon and trod plenty miles for dat."

"No, mon," Keverton laughed. "Not'ing like dat. Tacky want we to be him strong eyes."

"Him strong eyes?"

"Yes, mon. We have to watch de broad waters for any big boat dat come up."

"Dat's all him ask we to do?"

"It's very important, Moa. When me sleep, you watch, and when you sleep, me have to keep me eye open. Me hoping dat no big boat ah come up and dem just leave we alone."

"Me hope dat too," I said.

"And we have to check de dirt path dat lead down into Port Maria," added Keverton. "Some white mon down there might come up here so."

"And me have to do de same?"

"Yes, mon. Me nuh want any white mon coming up here so from de bush and killing we when we sleeping."

"So how long do we have to do dis?"

Keverton shrugged. "Me nuh know. Until Tacky

come back from de smaller plantation and tell we someting different."

"And if we do sight ah big boat, what are we supposed to do?"

"Run quicker than impatient breeze and let Tacky or Midgewood know. Or let Cornmon know. Him and ah few more cane warriors set up ah camp by de hill where we first look 'pon de wide blue waters. You remember, Moa, or you long sleep tek away you memory?"

I recalled the moment as if it had been just minutes ago. Midgewood had raised an arm as he crested a rise, and I'd gazed at the ocean for the very first time. It was spectacular.

"Yes, me remember it good," I said. "Me cyan never forget dat. Is there any food here so? Hungry me ah hungry."

Keverton's smile almost split his cheeks. "Yes, mon. Ah whole heap. There are vegetables and sugarcane and we have two chickens—Louis tek de rest of dem. Now you awake me cyan kill one, roast it, and eat it under de moon. What do you say to dat, Moa? Maybe we cyan watch de second night together? De dark waters look so mysterious at nighttime, especially when de fat moon shine 'pon it."

By the time the sun had sunk below the western ranges, Keverton had chopped off the head of a chicken and roasted it on a spit on the back lawn. My wound ached constantly. It reminded me of the pain I'd endured following Misser Donaldson's last whipping. At least this time, my agony was only in one place.

I managed to make it outside and join Keverton for supper under the stars. We had found some wooden bowls and mugs in another room that served as the kitchen. He was right—the ocean appeared as if it held many secrets beneath its waves. It looked beautiful with the streak of moonlight upon its rippling surface. I wondered: if we looked hard enough, would we be able to detect the Akan gods fishing out the souls of our brothers and sisters from the deep blue?

There was a small storeroom beside the kitchen that was full of vegetables and fruits. We enjoyed sweetsop, mango, and guava with our roast chicken. I thought of Miss Gloria, her smile and her rationed servings. An image of clean, gnawed-down chicken bones filled my head. I wondered what Mama, Hopie, Papa, and Hamaya would be eating tonight. *What are dem t'inking? Maybe dem asking Nyame, Asase Ya, and Bele Alua to protect me, Keverton, and de rest of we. Maybe more white mon come from ah different direction and lash dem against de long post. Maybe dem already in dem pits* . . . I shook my head to rid the picture from my mind.

I sensed the natural mystic. I imagined the Akan gods swirling around us. The cicadas and crickets came out to play. Along the coast to the east we could see the odd flash of light but it was too distant for Keverton and I to be too concerned. I concentrated my eyes on the shadowy seas, immense and broad before me. I couldn't detect a single movement upon its vast spread.

"Dis is too nice to be true," I said. "But one day de big boat will come."

Keverton nodded. "Me wish you would nuh mention dat, but dat's what Tacky say."

"And when it come," I added, "it'll be full of vexed white mon in strange pants and long jacket looking for dem revenge."

Keverton held my eyes for a while before nodding again. "De battle not over. So Tacky say."

"Let we hope dat de next battle is de final battle," I said.

Entranced by the waters, Keverton took awhile to answer me. "Moa," he said, "me just telling you dis for you good ears. Me nuh want to fight another battle. No, mon. Me would prefer to go to dis Dreamland where plenty fruit and vegetables cyan grow good and ripe, nuff rooster ah crow, plenty fat hog ah grunt, and then live good wid ah nice woman or two beside me. Dat's all me want to do."

"Two women beside you?" I laughed. "What happen to t'ree women? Dat's what me want to do too."

"And where you going to get de t'ree woman from?" Keverton asked.

"Dem will come to me for true."

Keverton bent up in mirth. "You have plenty ambition! Nuh tell Tacky me talking dis talk."

"Nuh worry youself, Keverton. Me won't tell him. We just talking and joking."

The chuckling faded and we gazed out to sea once again.

"War nuh pretty," Keverton said. "Old Misser Cliff dead, Cudgemon dead. Before dat dem kill off Pitmon and Miss Pam drop and gone. So we kill off plenty slavemaster, Misser Master, him wife, and him pickney."

I tried hard not to think about it.

"But me cyan see why," said Keverton. "Misser Master pickney kill off to save we own pickney."

"To stop dem troubling Hamaya and de rest of we pickney when dem reach dem size," I nodded. "To stop dem using dem back-ripper."

Keverton sat in silence for a long while. By the look of his expression, I guessed there was a battle taking place in his head. "Is dat how it must go?" he said finally. "Do we have to fight forever for just ah liccle piece of Dreamland? Why dem hate we so?"

"Me nuh know," I shook my head. "All me do know is dat me fighting for Mama, liccle Hopie, Hamaya, and de rest of dem."

"And if we carry on fighting, de white mon will t'ink twice or even t'ree times about troubling we," Keverton said.

"Isn't dat worth de fight?" I asked.

Keverton took a long pause before answering me. Then he nodded and blessed his eyes on me. "It is."

"Dat's what give me de strength," I said, "along wid Asase Ya, to kill Misser Donaldson. Me never t'ought me could do it."

"Me never even t'ink me coulda kill too," he admitted. "De warrior blood boil up inside of me at de Trinity plantation."

I watched Keverton stand up and take a few strides toward the sea. There he stood for a short while before returning. "Since we bruk out of de plantation," he said, "what tings fill you head?"

I thought about it. "Misser Donaldson's dead eyes," I replied. "Dat was de first ting. Him deat' look never leave me alone. Even now. Me t'ink of me mama, liccle Hopie, Papa, Hamaya, and even de pretty girl wid one foot. Me cyan't remember her name."

"Me t'ink of me mama too," said Keverton. "She dead not many seasons after me born. Romesha, dem called her. She gave birth to me at eighteen years old.

Me remember she look well pretty when de fat moon bless her face. Louis tell me she was more brown than black. Not too many words come outta her mout' but she try and help ever'body around her. Louis also tell me dat Miss Gloria did mind me when me was young and me have ah brudder who was taken away."

"Ah brudder?"

"Yes, mon. Four years older than me. Mama's first-born. Bullfrog, dem call him, becah him use to love jump over fence. Him was lighter-skinned than any other pickney. Yellow Bwoy, some people ah call him."

"Who was him papa?"

Keverton offered me a long look. "Misser Penceton. Mama wanted to kill sheself."

"Sorry to hear," I said. "Misser Penceton well brutal. De gods will never tek him spirit."

"Nobody know where dem tek me brudder," Keverton said. "One day him was killing de rats and picking out de weeds inna de cane field, de next day dem put him 'pon ah cart and him was gone. Mama bawl till de fat moon turn skinny. Becah me brudder's skin yellow, him might be living ah easier life. Me been t'inking dat one good day me might bless me eyes 'pon him."

"Dat would be ah good day," I said. "Maybe him will love him food just as much as you."

We both laughed hard. Keverton composed himself first. "But me nuh know who me papa is," he said.

"Me always wanted to ask you dat. Nobody tell you? Not even Louis? Maybe me mama know?"

Keverton shook his head. "No, mon. Me ask you mama one time and Miss Gloria, but dem nuh know either. Me mama never tell nobody."

"If you want to, you cyan borrow me own papa," I chuckled. "Me and him cyan't agree on anyting so maybe he cyan agree on someting wid you."

Keverton grinned and shook his head but decided not to comment.

"Whoever he is," I said, "he'll be mighty proud of you. Yes, mon. But all of we are sons of de land of Akan. Sons of de sky god Nyame and Him woman Asase Ya. So Tacky tell me so."

"Ah true. Him tell me de same ting. Louis tell me one day dat Tacky was ah king from de land of Akwamu. Yes, mon. Him nuh like to talk about it becah de white mon capture him and bring him here so."

"Ah king?" I said. "No lie you ah tell me? But now when me t'ink about it, him walk tall wid ah mighty head 'pon him shoulder. Him chin never rest 'pon him chest-top."

"Yes, Moa," Keverton replied. "Ah warrior king. He must fight de white mon or he will die in plenty shame. De Akan gods will nuh tek him soul if he nuh mek war. Ah terrible burden."

"We cyan't let dat happen," I said.

"Moa," Keverton smiled, "you nuh reach you full size yet but me proud of you."

"And me proud of you too."

Keverton wiped his forehead. "Me want you to know," he said, "me glad me wid you."

"Me well happy me wid you too. As long as you keep on giving me fair share of chicken and sweetsop."

"You could not complain if me give meself ah bigger portion—remember, me have two years 'pon you."

"But me need bigger piece to grow so me cyan reach you size," I laughed.

He stood up. "Me soon come. Me just going to check de dirt path. If me forget dat, Tacky will fling me down de mountainside. And me nuh want de John Crow to dig out me eye. Any slavemaster hiding there so will taste de sharp side of me blade."

He was gone for half an hour or so and when he returned, I felt a surge of relief. *Yes, it is good to have Keverton wid me. Me t'ank de Akan gods for dat liccle mercy.*

14

THE COASTAL CAVES

I'm not sure how many days Keverton and I spent at Fort Haldane. I was free but I missed everybody at the plantation, even my papa. I constantly prayed to the Akan gods, pleading with them to allow me to bless my eyes on my family again.

I wondered if Tacky, Midgewood, and the others had been successful in freeing the slaves from a third plantation. Now and again, somebody would come up from a watch camp about five miles away and tell us, "Everyting all right, nuh worry youself." They'd stop for something to eat and drink, take a long look at the ocean, and then they'd be gone again.

I did worry myself.

Every morning I rose with the sound of the rooster and peered into the yellow fields hoping to see my brothers' return.

My shoulder wound healed slowly but it left an ugly scar. It troubled me whenever I worked my right arm and I wondered how it would hold up in the hot rage of battle.

Keverton and I discussed many subjects but we never spoke of some things, like cutting sugarcane or the death mask of the white men we had killed. I had worked beside him for more than thirteen hours a day, but I had never heard him talk about finding a good woman and becoming a papa who will have plenty time to teach his children how to work the land and grow vegetables. We both wanted the same things. He told me that when the final fight was over, "You should go back to Trinity and claim de pretty girl wid de nice smile and de one foot. At least she cyan't run away from you!" He joked that he would build a big house with a staircase and have "t'ree women living wid me wid plenty pickney running about de place." It was nice discussing ambitions like that. In the cane field we only talked about keeping up our day's tally for Misser Master's satisfaction.

Sometimes we kept each other company on our night watches and we cooked meals together. We hadn't seen any sign of a white man trekking up the dirt path from Port Maria. One evening I put it to Keverton that maybe Tacky and his warriors had been killed. "Nuh, Moa!" Keverton raised his voice. "Nuh t'ink dat. Nyame and Asase Ya won't let dat happen. De gods walk wid dem."

We dared to dream that white men arriving on big boats would leave us alone and we'd be able to find a good piece of land to grow our own food and raise our own chickens and hogs.

One morning, I decided to trod farther afield to a co-conut grove, where I felled enough of the fruit to last us a moon cycle. I also picked a sackful of guinep ber-ries. When I returned, I spotted Tacky, Midgewood, Louis, Cornmon, Mooker, and many others in ani-mated conversation on the fort's back lawn. My heart wanted to reach them before my good foot did. I wondered how many more white men they had killed.

Four of them sat on the two black guns. There was much finger-jabbing and raised voices. As their de-bate intensified, they didn't spot my approach.

"Good to sight you!" I interrupted. "Everyting all right? What's de cuss-cuss about?"

"Cuss-cuss?" said Tacky. "Nobody cussing. What mek you t'ink dat?"

"But me hear you from back over there so," I said. "Somebody tek more chicken than dem should?"

"No, mon," Midgewood laughed. "We just decid-ing on someting."

"And what is dat someting?" I wanted to know.

"And before you give me an answer, me want to t'ank you for saving me good life. You cyan have de first coconut."

"Me cook for you almost every day and me nuh get de first coconut?" said Keverton.

I handed Midgewood the fruit and he licked his lips. Keverton feigned outrage.

"You have ah tough heart and skin t'ick like guango bark," Midgewood said. "But me well sorry me could nuh save Old Misser Cliff. Him passing still ah pain me and stop me sleeping at nighttime. He was de best of we. Nobody cyan sing de Akan song like Old Misser Cliff."

"He was de one who first made we t'ink to start de blood chant," said Louis.

"What chant was dat?" I asked.

"DE BLOOD REMEMBERS!" everyone hollered.

"Not one of we dead from de last plantation," Tacky said. "And Abowie mek sure nobody get hurt. It was ah small place. Dem only had twenty slaves. Dem could nuh believe it when dem sight we."

"We kill five of dem," revealed Midgewood. "Dem run off into de bush but dem foot not swift."

I wondered if Midgewood and the others were haunted in their dreams by white men's eyes like I was.

"So . . . what is dis someting?" I asked again. I

searched Keverton's eyes. He looked away. "Tell me nuh?"

Tacky gave me a long hard look before his expression softened. "All right, Moa, you have ah right to know."

"Ah right to know what?" I asked.

"We catch one of de white mon from Trinity," said Louis. "He was hiding inna de bush not too far from Trinity. Midgewood sight ah small fire one nighttime and dat lead we to him."

"We catch him and tie him up," said Louis. "Once we t'ump up him face and brutalize him body, him was ready to talk."

"What is de problem?" I asked.

"Him tell we somebody get away 'pon ah horse as soon as we attack Trinity," Tacky revealed. "The masser's brudder—Misser Bannion, dem call him. And him ride to ah place dat dem call Spanish Town. Spanish Town ah big place wid plenty big buildings. Nuff white mon there so. Dem probably have ah wagonload ah musket—and dem musket coming for we."

A rush of something cold filled my head and flowed through the rest of my body. It found its way to my feet. I stared at the ground.

"And de white mon we catch want we to put down we muskets and long knife and go back to work on de cane," said Midgewood. "Him laugh and him laugh and him say de English will send army after we and kill all of we."

I glanced at Keverton. *He will have to wait ah liccle longer to build him big cabin wid de long staircase for him t'ree women and pickney.*

"What . . . what did you do?" I asked.

"Mooker get vex and kill him wid one strike of him billhook," said Tacky. "And chop off him dutty tongue. Mooker did nuh want to waste time about what we should do wid him."

Mooker nodded but didn't say anything. I could never tell what he was thinking.

"Will . . . will dem march from Spanish Town to here so?" I asked.

Tacky shook his head. "No, mon. White mon nuh like to trod t'rough bush and over hill. Dem toe get too tired and de fly love dem beards. Dem will come by de broad waters."

I glanced out to the ocean. It was perfectly still, a crystal blue. It sparkled here and there.

"Dem might leave we alone," I said. "Dem might not want to fight we."

Tacky shook his head. "No, mon. All of we are worth ah big boatload of money to dem. Dem cyan't leave we alone. Dem need we to cut de cane, and if we cyan't do dat for dem, dem will kill we and look for more slaves. Dem will never leave we free if we nuh tek up we stance before dem."

"We have to fight dem," said Midgewood. "And try and stop dem coming up to Trinity and Frontier. Me nuh want dem to trouble we women and pickney again. No, mon. Me nuh live inna de wild bush for untold moons to see dat happen."

"So, me give you de choice again, Moa," Tacky said. "You cyan go back to Frontier if you want to. You mama will smile de broadest smile yet when she sight you. And you papa will nuh look 'pon me like him want to kill and dig ah pit for me. You fight ah good fight already. You de youngest cane warrior among we and de long musket almost tek away you life once already. It's ah sign. De Akan gods smiling at you and dem want you to live. Yes, mon. Me must listen to dat message."

"We have to stay here so and wait for de white mon to come," said Midgewood. "And dem will come . . . any day now."

"Young you ah still young," added Tacky. "We cyan't ask you to do any more."

I considered my options. Everyone's gaze was on me. I remembered what Midgewood said before, and thought, *Me haven't killed white mon, trod plenty miles, and suffer from long gun blasting me down only to step back to de plantation. No, mon!*

I thought of Mama, Papa, Hopie, Hamaya, and the pretty girl with one foot. Part of me so much wanted to return to them, but not without Keverton. He was only two years older than me. *We cut de cane together, live together, quarrel together, and fight together. Me cyan't leave him now.*

"No, mon," I said finally. "You need as much black hand dat you cyan find to help conquer de white mon army. Me fighting for more than me good self. Me fighting for de Hamayas and de liccle Hopies dat not even born yet."

"Awwurra!" cried Midgewood.

Tacky studied me silently. "All right," he said after a moment. "But when de battle gets too hot you must tek up you good foot and go'way. You nuh grow to you full size yet. No white mon cyan catch you wid dem heavy foot. You toes will always be swifter than dem."

"Me will never run away," I said.

"Him nuh tek off him quick foot and leave me yet," said Keverton, smiling at me. "Brave him brave. Maybe too much courage ah flow t'rough him body. His blood remember him warrior ancestors for true."

Something crunched and twisted inside my stomach. *Me not dat brave. Me just want to be beside Keverton. Dat's all. Me feel safe wid him next to me.*

"While you talk about how tough Moa's heart is," said Cornmon, "cyan me have some white coconut?"

I shook all the fruit out of my sack and my brothers gratefully picked them up. Eating and drinking the berries and coconut milk relaxed the serious eyes around me, although it didn't settle the new storm in my stomach. As I refreshed myself, Tacky snatched glances at me. I suspected that he wasn't telling me everything.

"Are we going down to de caves or not?" asked Louis. "Me want to go down there and cool me foot inna de waters."

"De caves?" I said. "What is dat?"

My question was ignored. I hated it when they did that to me. *Me not have grown to me full size but me not ah pickney no more!*

Midgewood took the lead and everyone followed. I walked with Keverton and whispered to him, "What are these caves dat Louis talking about?"

"Ah . . . ah place by de blue waters. Ah spiritual place to go to. Dem say it kinda mysterious there so. Tacky find it ah few days ago. Him been spending time praying there wid Midgewood and Scallion Mon."

We headed west through a field of wild grass before hacking our way through tangled bushes and bramble. For a good while we trekked inland, but eventually our course bent right toward the sea again. My shoulder wound throbbed once more. My blisters reopened. The land descended steadily. The under-growth was damp and matted and the air was thick. We soon approached a brook. Its trickling waters gave life to long thin reeds and arching skinny trees with wide leaves that blocked the sunlight. The mudbanks were smooth and slippery. Tiny insects buzzed and crawled around the tree roots. Mosquitoes bred in damp mud patches and still waters. Birds, showing off their bright colors and long tails, sang above us. Small green lizards hopped here and there.

Brothers hummed an Akan song that I remembered my mama singing to me when I was small:

Nuh worry, children,
Slavemaster have no god friend.
You always drop to you bed,
You back bruk again,
But nuh worry, children,
Slavemaster have no god friend.
We ancestors survive de long blue.
Dem watch we smallest pickney grow true.

Still breathing after blistered pirates plant we
'pon cane field
Where greedy iron eats ankle bone
And back-ripper mek proud black turn red.
De all of we still not dead

So nuh worry, children,
Slavemaster have no god friend.

Never forget we warrior Queen Nanny
Or de stories of Anancy.
Nyame and Asase Ya will guide we good foot
And bring we back to mama tree root.
So nuh worry, children,
Slavemaster have no god friend.

Suddenly an opening appeared in the bush and soft white sand was beneath my feet. The perfect blue sea stretched out to meet the sky and I squinted as the full force of sunlight hit my face. We pulled off our shoes and stepped into the gentle lapping waters. My blisters stung but I was grateful for the cool sensation soothing my legs. I could've stayed there forever.

For the next half an hour or so, Tacky allowed us to relax, drink coconut milk, and splash ourselves as he, Midgewood, and Louis resumed their debate on the beach. It was one of those rare times when I saw my brothers smiling. We talked about our Dreamland where we would raise families and even more chickens and goats. I imagined sitting around a fire as an old man telling my grandchildren Anancy stories that I learned from Miss Pam.

Midgewood called us in and led us westward toward a gray-brown rock formation that protruded out into the sea. It seemed strange to my eye surrounded by so much rich green. We had to wade into the waters thigh-high to reach a thin, S-shaped opening into the caves. The occasional stone lying on the seabed bruised my blisters. Thick green-brown weeds clung to the sea-washed rocks at its mouth, and a blue-blackness hugged the inside walls. Underfoot, the sand was brown-yellow and cool to the touch. The air was fresher, and birds had made their nests in high corners. A long insect with pincers bigger than its head scuttled along the ground on business of its own. Other small hidden creatures screeched their strange screeches. The breath of the ocean was amplified inside, and when Tacky spoke, his voice seemed deeper, as if it came from somewhere far away. *Maybe dat's how dem sound in Akwamu land.* I imagined my ancestors watching me.

"Sit down, me brudders," Tacky said.

We did what we were told and arranged ourselves in a circle. Keverton placed his hand on my shoulder. "If you want to," he said, "you cyan go back and enjoy de nice waters. Dis not meant for you good ears."

"No, mon," I replied. "Me want to hear what Tacky have to say."

As before, Tacky approached each of us and studied our eyes. He regarded me longer than anyone else.

I was glad he couldn't see my thumping heart. For a short moment I thought he was about to instruct us to build a boat and set sail to the land of our mothers. *Nuh be foolish, Moa. De only one who know about building tings wid wood is Old Misser Cliff and him talking to we ancestors right now.*

Then Tacky climbed onto a rock at the back of the cave and looked down on us. We stood in a semicircle and gazed up at him.

"De white mon is coming to kill we," said Tacky. "So when dem come we will meet dem in battle. But remember dis: de hotter de battle, de sweeter de victory."

"Awwurra!"

"We cyan't let dem get close to we women and pickney," Tacky went on. "No, mon! We will tek we position 'pon de hill beside de path dat lead to Trinity. Me want to see dem coming."

"How . . . how many of dem you t'ink will come?" asked a freedom fighter.

Tacky stood tall and still. I imagined him wearing rich garments and a crown upon his head. He considered his reply. "Me cyan't tell you how many will come. But what me cyan tell you is dat you courage, tough heart, and strong hand mek me chest swell wid pride."

"And we proud of you too!" yelled Louis.

"And we have Nyame and Asase Ya to guide we," Scallion Mon raised his voice.

"*Awwurra!*"

"Remember," Tacky continued, "too many times we had to watch white mon come inna de middle of de night and tek we women. We lost too many under de white mon back-ripper. When we work inna de field, de John Crow fly above we expecting we to drop for dem next dinner. Too much pit we had to dig. We just bury Old Misser Cliff ah short while ago—mek him spirit return to de Akan gods. But de blood remembers."

"DE BLOOD REMEMBERS!" repeated the warriors. "DE BLOOD REMEMBERS!"

Tacky nodded his approval. "So, me mighty cane warriors, me want to ask you someting."

"Ask you question!" called out Midgewood.

"DE BLOOD REMEMBERS!"

"If even we lose de next battle," Tacky said loudly, "if we alive, who want to go back to de hot sting of de back-ripper and de John Crow flying above you headtop waiting for you to drop?"

"NONE OF WE!" chanted everyone.

"Me never hear you," said Tacky. "Who want to go back?"

I almost burst my lungs in response. "NONE OF WE!"

"Awwurra!"

The call and response went on for a few minutes. Men stamped their feet and slapped the walls. Birds took flight. Tacky and Midgewood stood still, soaking up our brotherhood and strength.

"Dis is de place me want you to come to if de battle get too hot," Tacky said after a while. "If we listen carefully, we cyan hear de tongue of de broad waters. Yes, mon. And across de wide blue is where we come from. We cyan't see it but me know it's there. Ah place of black kings and queens. Ah place where liccle pickney rise in de morning and look forward to playing tee-tah-toe. Yes, mon. Believe it. Dem will never tek we alive again."

"NEVER!" chanted Midgewood.

"All right, me mighty cane warriors," said Tacky, "you know what you have to do if de battle get too hot. Mek we go back now and prepare for when dem come. But dis is ah good place. We ancestors from across de long blue will sense you spirits from here so."

15

TACKY'S OATH

Tacky had set up two watch camps on the dirt track between Fort Haldane and Trinity plantation. Keverton and I were instructed to maintain our watch at Fort Haldane and to always trod with our billhooks. I asked Tacky for a long musket but he denied me. "Every mon who have ah gun have grown to dem full size," he said.

We were warned constantly not to fall asleep at the same time. Midgewood was the last cane warrior to leave our watchhouse but before he did so, he presented us with two chickens. "To keep you belly happy and you tired eye open," he said. "Remember, when you sight someting, me there wid Cornmon at de first watch camp. Nuh let you foot rest 'pon de ground for too long."

That night, Keverton and I dined on roast chicken,

guinep berries, and coconut pulp as we peered out to the dark seas. I was too anxious and overloaded with dread to sleep.

We sat in silence for a while before I raised what troubled me. "What does Tacky mean when him say we will never be tek alive?"

Keverton didn't turn his face to look at me. The broad waters held his gaze as if he were expecting the duppies of our lost brothers and sisters to rise out of it.

"Keverton," I pressed again.

"He mean what him say," he finally answered. "When you were looking for coconut, we swore to de Akan gods dat we will never return to slavery. No, mon. And if we lose de final battle, any of we who survive . . . will tek we own life. Everyone swore to Nyame and Asase Ya to dat. Scallion Mon mek sure of dat. Him look hard at every mon eye. Dat oath cyan never bruk."

"Tek we own life?" I repeated. Something other than my heart beat within me. Terror, fear, and the prospect of loss. The wound I had sustained pained me again. Suddenly my legs became weak. *How cyan me tek me own life?*

Keverton turned to face me. "But not you, Moa," he said. "Young you ah still young. Tacky say you nuh grow to you full size yet. One good day you might be longer and broader than me."

"But me cyan fight as good as de next mon," I argued.

"Yes, you cyan," Keverton nodded. "But as Tacky see it, him nuh want you to swear to de Akan gods to tek you own life. Me was wid Tacky on dat argument. Midgewood say you old and brave enough, but him was chanted down."

"Midgewood right," I said. "Me will swear to de gods in me own good time."

Keverton shook his head. "Me tell Midgewood you would nuh listen to him, me, or nobody else, becah you have you own mind to decide what to do. Anyway, big trouble is coming to we. If de gods keep we hand strong, no mon will have to tek him own life. Grayness will mark you headtop, de creases next to you eyes will grow plenty like rings inna tree trunk. You will sight many more fat and skinny moons."

Keverton stood up and switched his gaze to the ocean once again. "Me nuh have by me side no blood brudder, sister, mama, or papa. Moa, you de nearest ting me have to dat. Dat's why me want you to live no matter what happen. What did Tacky tell me? If you live for youself you live in vain, if you live for somebody else you live again. Nuh worry about me, Moa. Nuh matter what happen, me will live again. Me believe dat for true."

"Me want you to live today and tomorrow," I replied. "And de good days after dat. You only two years older than me. And you cyan still have you big house wid de staircase, de t'ree women, and ah whole heap of pickney running about de place."

"Tacky give you ah choice becah you nuh reach full size yet," Keverton said. "And nobody will judge you. But me have grown to me full size . . . me know what me have to do."

He smiled and turned to leave. I watched him disappear along the dirt path. My tears ran down over my chin and onto my neck. I closed my eyes and thought about death. The very idea of it released aches inside of me. *Maybe me too young for true becah why me dread it so much?* I hoped it wasn't too painful. I imagined meeting my ancestors and wondered how they'd receive me. I prayed they'd be proud of me. *Yes, me ready . . . or as ready as me cyan ever hope to be.*

16

THE BIG BOATS

Five days later, there was a pretty sunset. Gold and pink kissed the edges of the clouds. It was an unusual moment when all thoughts of vexed white men coming to kill me had retreated to a small corner in the back of my mind. Keverton had told me that Tacky and Midgewood were marching between Trinity, Frontier, and lookout camps preparing for the final battle. I tried hard not to listen.

We both marveled at the amber glow reflecting upon the darkening waters. A keen wind refreshed us from the north and it disturbed the bushes and trees around us. It whistled through the long grass and drowned out whatever dispute the crickets and cicadas were having. A cool Jamaican evening.

We had just enjoyed a meal of leftover chicken back, chicken claws, vegetables, and herbs that Keverton had boiled to make a broth. We washed it down with water that I had collected from a nearby stream. There was a nice, warm sensation in my stomach as I leaned back and studied the heavens. *Maybe we cyan get to live good and nuh worry about white mon troubling we. Maybe me cyan find de pretty girl wid one foot and build ah pretty cabin to live in. Maybe me could have two pickney or even t'ree. Me will tell dem Anancy story to mek dem laugh.*

"Moa! Moa!" Keverton called. "Nuh close you eye yet!"

I sat up, blinked, and focused my attention toward the sea. I spotted two sets of white sails coming in from the west. The ships silently cut through the water and were close to shore. They left thin white trails in their wake. For a short moment I admired the sight, and then I wondered how objects so big could float on the broad blue without sinking.

Keverton stood up. "Dem ah come," he said. "Dem ah come for we."

Cold dread coursed through my bones.

"Put out de fire!" Keverton ordered.

I stamped out the fire and ran to fetch my billhook and two water coconuts I had in my room. Keverton collected his long musket. We ran outside again and stood on the black cannons to look. *Me wish somebody could teach me how to fire dem. Me would sink de big boats for true.* We peered out to sea one last time.

Two big boats headed for Port Maria. Someone had lit fires on the beach. Shadows moved in the distance. We heard faraway urgent voices.

"Two of dem," Keverton said. "Dem must carry nuff white mon. Come, Moa. Ready you foot."

We barely stopped for breath as we ran up hills, swift-footed into valleys, and leaped over ditches to the first watch camp. I found it hard to keep up as Keverton long-strode ahead of me. He scrambled up a steep slope as I took a short rest. As I finally crested the rise, Keverton had already given a quick report to Midgewood and Cornmon. Twenty more cane warriors, sitting around a small fire and eating a late dinner, listened in. I looked for Tacky but couldn't find him. He had picked a good spot to surprise an army. It offered a high view of the bending lands before the coast and we could hide ourselves behind shoulders and folds of the rolling hills. Dense woodland rose sharply to the west of us.

Midgewood dispatched two fighters into the bush to carry the news. I sat down to take another breather and refreshed myself with a water coconut. My upper body ached once more and my blisters had reopened. It was then that I noticed Cornmon and his company had been busy. Lying on the ground underneath the cover of the trees were dozens and dozens of sharpened wooden spikes about a man and a half long. I walked over and picked up one. They had been stripped of their bark and were smooth to hold. I felt the point and it pricked my thumb. A thin trail of blood ran over my knuckle. *Nuff blood ah go run tonight.*

Keverton came over, collected one of the spikes, and said, "We're going to fight dem here so."

"We are?" I replied.

He pointed to the dirt path. "Dem will come t'rough here so. And when dem do, we'll attack dem from de bush. Midgewood say dem will be expecting to fight we at Trinity or Frontier."

"Where's Tacky?" I asked.

"He's at de second camp."

I breathed easier.

"It's where dem keeping we food, water, goats, and ting," Keverton added. "All of dem will soon come here so. Dis is de last battle, Moa."

"How . . . how soon do you t'ink dem will come?" I pressed.

"Nuh worry, Moa," Keverton said. "Him not too far away."

The fires were put out and fighters tried to destroy any evidence that there had been a camp here. Tacky arrived half an hour later or so with a band of fifty men. Some of them I didn't recognize. Then I remembered Tacky had raided a third plantation.

One of these new warriors chanted strange words at the heavens. He had untamed hair and wore a necklace of bones. There was no escaping his hypnotic gaze. He ground a white powder in a wooden bowl, then sprinkled and dabbed everyone's faces and hands with it. It failed to instill any more confidence in me, but it seemed to offer many warriors renewed bravery.

"*Awwurra!*" they chanted.

"DE BLOOD REMEMBERS!"

I wiped my cheek with my finger, examined the white dust, and asked Keverton, "What . . . what is dis?"

"It's ah spell." He didn't seem sure. "De obeahmon say it'll protect we from de white mon muskets."

"Obeahmon?"

"Yes, Moa. One of dem come up from de small plantation. Obeahmon cyan speak wid de Akan gods and listen to dem. Dem de messengers. Nobody play wid dem or mek dem vex becah dem afraid dem might get curse. Dem cyan kill ah mon wid one long look."

"Me wish dem coulda paint me face wid white powder before me get shot up ah Fort Haldane," I said.

"And me pray dem coulda color me wid de powder before Misser Donaldson first season me wid him back-ripper," said Keverton. "De Akan gods shoulda mek him come alive so me cyan kill him again."

We managed to raise a half smile.

Tacky ordered us into two long rows set up in a position just inside the woods. The dirt path was a hundred strides away. Those who bore arms were placed in the first line of defense. I was reluctant to leave Keverton's side but Midgewood argued me into obedience.

"It'll be all right, Moa," Keverton said. "Tomorrow we'll be eating chicken and sweetsop again around ah fire."

Tacky came along and slapped my back. He gave me a long, proud look. "You heart strong, Moa, but remember what me tell you: know you size."

I didn't feel any better. Fear gripped and chewed my insides. Tears dripped down my cheeks. *We live together, we cut de cane together, we eat together, kill together . . .*

I lay flat on the ground with my billhook in my right hand and a wooden spike in the other. I wondered what white man might find himself on the killing end of either weapon. *Will de next gunshot rip t'rough me heart? Who will be lef' standing to dig me pit? And Old Misser Cliff no longer here to chant me ah nice chant.*

I heard every bird in the treetops, felt every gust of wind against my face, and my heartbeat punched the ground beneath me. Keverton kneeled thirty yards ahead of me. It may as well have been thirty miles. He trained his musket at an unseen enemy. Deep night soon closed all around us. Untold stars filled the heavens.

I wondered if I'd bless my eyes on another dawn. The only voices I heard were Tacky's, Midgewood's, and an army of cicadas. The north breeze suddenly stilled. My shirt stuck to my skin and I felt the weight of it upon my shoulders.

About an hour later, a warrior walked along our lines of defense and offered us coconut water and berries. "De white mon might not come until morning time," he said.

I prayed that they wouldn't come at all.

I could hardly swallow the juice. I wasn't sure if my stretched nerves could tolerate waiting through the night for the battle to begin. It was a comfort to see Keverton glancing back at me every now and again. I tried to gain strength from it.

17

THUNDERING GROUND

I couldn't count the hours that long, dark night, but as I woke, I'll never forget how the very earth echoed and resonated beneath me. It was as if there was a giant heart beating in the core of the world.

"Dem ah come!" someone cried aloft in a tree. "And dem ah come 'pon horse."

I stood up and could see a red dawn spreading from the east. The hills formed dull, green shapes in the early morning light. The odd bird chirped above. My fingers trembled around my billhook and spike. I took in a quick breath and exhaled for a long moment. The ache in my shoulder pulsed hard. My throat felt as dry as a fallen, crinkled leaf.

"Nuh fire till dem come over de hill," Tacky commanded.

"*Awwurra!*"

I heard the distant drum of galloping hooves and vengeful war cries. I looked around and called out: "Keverton!"

He glanced over his shoulder. "Get flat!" he ordered me. "Get you body flat!"

I desperately wanted to join him in battle but remained where I lay. I studied the faces of the warriors around me. Some stared ahead grimly, while three, including Scallion Mon, offered prayers to the Akan gods. Others looked at Tacky and Midgewood for inspiration.

Fighters with arms took to one knee and trained their guns at the dirt path. The ground vibrated beneath us. The red morning marched on. The peaks of the distant hills were capped in a pink mist.

"Ready!" shouted Tacky. "Asase Ya is wid we!"

Gunmen fingered their triggers and adjusted their positions. Sweat drenched my brows. I squeezed my hand around my billhook but developed a cramp in my forefinger. A picture of Mama and little Hopie gatecrashed my mind. Hamaya was there too. *Me have to try and defend dem. Me nuh want dem to ride up to de plantation and trouble dem.*

"*Awwurra!*" Scallion Mon yelled.

"*AWWURRA!*"

The riders came.

Untold hooves thundered up and over the hill. Several horsemen held fire torches. They wore blue jackets, white pants, and black boots. Their beards scratched their collarbones.

"Fire your muskets!" Tacky cried.

The noise deafened me. Horses reared and screamed, their forelegs fighting the air. Some fell to the ground with a mighty thud. They kicked up a swirl of brown dust as riders tried to remount. Cries and shrieks ricocheted around me. I couldn't see that far ahead but Keverton was still there on one knee. He desperately tried to reload his gun. Mooker was the first to break ranks. He charged ahead and Tacky went with him. "DE BLOOD REMEMBERS!"

The cloud of dust soon veiled them. Musket against musket. Sharp steel carved muscle and split bones. Wood crashed against jaw.

"Form a line!" I heard a white man shout. "Form a line and fire at will!"

I'll never forget the sound of that volley of gunfire. Someone lying beside me just sprang to his feet and, driven by mad fear, bolted into the woods. He left his billhook behind. I heard Papa's voice in my head willing me to escape—but not without Keverton. Brothers fell in front of me. Their dying masks would haunt me until the day Death dropped me in its handcart. *Asase Ya? Where are you? Nyame? Bele Alua?*

Broken cheeks, shattered noses, smashed skulls, and stomachs spilling whatever was inside of them. Smoke filled the air. The crash and clamor of weapon against flesh was all about me. The stench of organs and ripped limbs rose from the ground. *Why me still alive? Maybe de obeahmon's powder is working?*

I looked for Keverton but couldn't find him. Kicked-up soil and gun smoke obscured my vision. I jumped to my feet, gripped my billhook and spike, and lunged forward.

Smoke cleared.

I spotted a white man very close to me. For a short moment our eyes connected in a shared panic. He was about to reload his long musket but I didn't give him the opportunity. I drove my spike deep into his chest and hacked his neck with my billhook. His blood spattered my face. He fell instantly. "*Awwurra!*"

My blood boiled within me. I didn't know which way to turn. Long knives rose and fell. Screams, dust, and confusion disorientated me.

"Tacky gone!" a warrior cried. "Tacky dead and gone!"

It was a mournful shout, drained of all confidence. Something emptied out of my willing spirit.

"Tacky dead and gone!"

A defeated wail.

For a stretched moment I was unable to move as

the howl seeped into my bones and into my veins.

"Tacky dead and gone!"

I refused to believe it. *Asase Ya walks wid him.*

Doubt gave away to rage. I blindly chopped and hacked all around me. Gunshots continued to bruise my ears. Another white man fell in front of me, but I couldn't tell if it was by my own hand.

Suddenly a firm palm gripped my shoulder. Hard fingers dug into my flesh. My entire body went rigid. *Is dis de moment of me deat'?* I snapped my head to my left. It was Keverton. Grime, blood, and sweat mingled with the white powder upon his face. He looked at me hard and only said two words: "Come, Moa."

I didn't need a second invitation. He led me into the high woods.

"But . . . but what about Tacky and Midgewood?" I said.

Keverton's hand was strong. He didn't reply.

As we clambered up an almost vertical rise, I noticed that he'd been wounded in his left leg. The boots that he had stolen from one of the dead guards at Fort Haldane were now spotted in fresh blood. I saw him wince and grimace as we ascended.

"If me stop," he said, "you must forward on. Agony licking me from me toe corner to me headtop."

"Me not stepping forward widout you," I said.

He bared his teeth, squinted in pain, and pushed

ahead once more. I felt guilty because I wasn't strong enough to carry him. When he faltered, I pulled him up with me. I used the skinny trunks of trees to haul us upward. Gunpowder and the scent of the earth filled my nostrils. The battle raged below but I didn't dare look behind.

"Tek . . . tek off me shirt," Keverton said.

I helped him pull off his top garment. Perspiration dripped down his whip-scarred back. *Somebody like Misser Donaldson really should be killed twice.*

"Now fix it tight around me leg," he ordered. "You must stop de flow of de blood—so me hear Miss Pam tell ah wounded brudder."

I did what I was told. His blood stained my fingers. He yelped in pain as I tied the knot. He was unable to move his left leg freely but he didn't shriek as loud as he had before.

We pulled ourselves higher. Our fingers clawed the ground. Tree roots bruised my knees and ankles. The trees gave way to thick bush and stiff shrubs as we dragged ourselves forever onward. Thorns and sharp twigs tormented my cheeks. Yard by yard. Inch by inch. The thick air suffocated me. Sweat blurred my vision. I checked on Keverton and his eyes were closing. *Oh no.*

"Nuh dead 'pon me here so, Keverton," I pleaded. "Becah me nuh know which way to go. Me want to see you big house wid de long staircase and look 'pon you pretty women. Me want to play tee-tah-toe wid you pickney. And me want you to tell dem Anancy stories from de land of we mudders."

He smiled with his lips but not his eyes. "Me cyan't climb no more, Moa," he said. "Let me rest. Nuh worry youself. Me won't dead 'pon you."

His eyes flickered then closed. I boxed him hard on his forehead to make sure he hadn't died on me.

"Moa! You want to kill me?"

I glanced over my shoulder and was relieved that we had found generous cover. Broad green leaves hung over us. I dared to stand up. Far below, white men tended to their perished and wounded. Dead black bodies littered the scarred and smoking ground. Their final resting poses weren't pretty. *Me brudders.* As I ducked under the canopy, I couldn't stop my tears. *Where Tacky there so? Midgewood? Mooker? Louis? Cornmon, Scallion Mon, and de rest of we cane warrior? Where Nyame, Asase Ya, and de mighty Bele Alua? Why dem never save me brudders?*

18

SEPARATION

I'm not sure if it was shock that claimed me or sheer exhaustion, but I found myself waking up as the sun dipped beyond the western hills. Keverton wasn't with me. I stood up and frantically searched the immediate area. "Keverton! Keverton! Where you there so?"

No answer.

Why him lef' me? Me nuh know which way to go. Lost me lost!

Moments later, something rustled above. It was him. I let out a long sigh and my heartbeat slowed. He was bare-chested. Back-ripper scars almost completely covered his back. His top garment, stained with his own blood, was still secured around his left leg. He moved with a limp but a little easier than he did during our flight. He carried a handful of yellow berries. When he spotted me, he grinned. "It seem like every time we have ah battle," he said, "sleep catch you at de end of it."

"How . . . how long me been sleeping?" I asked.

Keverton shrugged. "Me nuh know. Me wake up and find you sleeping next to me."

There was something odd about him. I sensed it in his eyes.

"You must hold you tongue, Moa," Keverton warned. "White mon about. And dem have broad ears and itchy musket fingers"

"Sorry, me t'ought you lef' me." I took two berries and ate them quickly. I stared at Keverton but he looked away. "Tacky?" I said.

"You want someting to drink?"

"Midgewood?"

"We nuh eat someting good for ah long time now," he said. "We have to look for ah goat or ah chicken inna de bush or try to find Midgewood's place up inna de hills."

"Keverton!" I raised my voice. "What . . . what happen?"

He dropped his head and gazed at the ground. For a few moments, all I heard was his breathing rhythm. When he raised his face again, it was full of tears. I had never seen him weep before. His lips twitched and his mouth opened. He struggled to find words.

This picture of Keverton will never leave me until the Akan gods collect me. "Dem gone," he finally said. "Only ah few survive. May de gods protect dem spirit."

"Tacky?" I said. "Me hear ah cane warrior cry dat him dead and gone but someting inna me heart say him survive."

Keverton closed his eyes for a long time. When he finally opened them he shook his head.

"Midgewood?"

He dipped his head again, wiped his face with the back of his hand, and ate another berry. "The obeah-mon dead too. Maybe de gods wanted ah sacrifice. Dem will live again."

"How . . . how many survive?" I asked.

"Me sight seven mon up inna de hills. Me nuh know about anyone else."

"Where dem now?"

Keverton ignored my question. "We have to look for some water coconut or someting," he said. "You have to build up you strength again."

"Where dem gone?"

"If you nuh ask me no question, me cyan't tell you no lie."

"But . . ."

"But not'ing, Moa. We have to climb where de mist hug de mountaintop. As me just say, white mon wid long musket still about. And dem ears cyan work just as good as we own."

We climbed up another sheer slope, pulling ourselves up by bush roots, stiff grass, and hard clumps of dry earth. The air became thinner. I glanced down into the valley. The dirt track looked like a brown ribbon cutting through the green of the land. The hills in the east were turning gray-blue. The breeze had come alive again but this time it blew from the west. The ache in my shoulder wound had spread to my neck and lower back. My blisters seeped.

At last we heaved ourselves over a ridge and rolled onto a narrow bank of long pale grass. Trees and shrubs grew horizontally above us. We lay on our backs for a few minutes to rest our spent bodies. I could just make out half a sun sinking below the western ranges. The light faded fast. Nothing was said. I imagined the spirits of my dead brothers soaring to the heavens. I heard them chanting: *De blood remembers! Awwurra!*

After a long while, Keverton rose to his feet and disappeared into the bush. *Where him find de strength? Maybe Asase Ya bless him wid it.* I was too exhausted to follow him. The images of my fallen brothers kept rolling through my mind. Tacky, Midgewood, Mooker, Louis, Cornmon, Scallion Mon, Old Misser Cliff, Cudgemon, and Pitmon. *All of dem dead.*

Maybe Papa was right. Maybe me shoulda stayed at de plantation. Me good heart cyan't tek dis.

Half an hour later, Keverton returned with two water coconuts. I had no idea how he had come about them in the dark. He tossed me one and I broke it against a skinny tree root. I drank greedily from it. It was cool, and as it hit my throat, I thought it was the best I had ever tasted.

"So where do we tek we good foot now?" I asked. "Maybe we could go down to de valley and bury we brudders?"

Silence.

"You nuh hear me, Keverton? Me say where should we trod now? Maybe white mon still down there so and we cyan't bury we brudders yet."

Keverton turned to face me. "Yes," he said. "Me check 'pon dem earlier when you were catching sleep. Ah few of dem set up camp and dem cooking someting."

"So which way should we trod?" I wanted to know. "Me wish Midgewood was wid we. Him would know. Maybe we should wait for morning?"

He stared at the ground again and took in a few long breaths. He lifted his head and met my gaze.

"Keverton? Someting wrong?"

"Dis is where we good foot must walk inna different direction," he said. He grimaced as if these words pained him. His jaw muscles danced.

It took a few seconds for his words to hit my nerves. A cold fear washed over my heart. Suddenly my head felt hot.

"Me nuh know what you mean," I replied. "We survive. We must look for some food now. Maybe try and find we way back to Midgewood's place."

Keverton shook his head. "You nuh listen, Moa. You have hard ears."

"Me nuh listen to what?"

"Mek you way back to Frontier," he said. "Sight you mama and liccle Hopie again. Say *Wo ho te sen* to fierce Hamaya."

"Not widout you," I said.

He sucked in a long intake of breath. His chest expanded. "Me swore to de Akan gods. Promise me ah promise dem. Ever'body hear me and me nuh want to bruk it. Me have to honor Tacky, Midgewood, and Scallion Mon. Me will live again."

I knew what he meant. My heart banged inside me. "You cyan't leave me here so."

I didn't notice it before but there was a billhook lying in the grass. Keverton picked it up. He looked at me as only a brother could. He pointed south. "Stay 'pon high ground," he said. "But keep heading dat way when morning light come. Keep de dirt track in sight but nuh step too close to it. White mon down there and dem will shoot you down. And dem will tek you dead body, chop off you head, and show it to you mama. Dem won't dig no pit for you and no Akan song will chant. No long tree will look over you. Evil dem ah evil. None of we want to be tied up by long post and let back-ripper do its work."

I had to take a moment to digest his words as something crunched in my stomach. I put on my warrior face. "But me going wid you," I said.

Keverton turned and hobbled away. I ran to join him, but as soon as I caught up with him he punched me to the ground with a mighty fist. My head felt like a cracked coconut. I had double vision for a moment and a tingly sensation in my legs. I shook my head and tried to blink the shock away.

"Moa!" Keverton shouted. "Listen to what me say! Forward to Midgewood's place when de sun rise. You will find ah goat and ting there."

He set off again. His left foot shuffled along the ground. *Why him ah treat me so bad? We grow together, eat together, sometime Misser Donaldson whip we together.*

My legs were unsteady, but I finally managed to take my stance again. I chased after him. *Boof.* He struck me on the back of my head with the handle of his billhook. I fell to the ground once more. This time, I couldn't get up.

"Listen to me, Moa." Keverton's voice was breaking and stuttering with crushing pain. His lips wobbled. "Nuh tek away me chance of joining me ancestors. Me will live again t'rough you. Fallen fighters will rise again, so Tacky say so. We'll tek we mighty stance again. And one good day, we'll back de evil against de wall. Tek up you good foot and look for you mama, liccle Hopie, and Hamaya. Live for dem."

19

ALONE

Sometime later, I managed to get to my feet. Night was still king but I couldn't see the stars above me. It was then that I realized I had slipped into the bush again. Sleep must've caught me. A water coconut and a handful of berries were resting next to my head. A billhook was waiting for me on my other side. I sat up and wept. Then I cried some more. My shoulder throbbed. *He swore to tek him own life.* A picture of the coastal caves and the sound of the blue waves slapping against their entrance filled my mind.

There I stayed until the gray light of morning touched the horizon. I ate berries and washed them down with coconut water. I prayed to hear the rustling of Keverton approaching with his long strides but knew the Akan gods wouldn't allow it. He had already promised them.

How cyan me forward in dis life widout him? Me spend more time beside him than anyone else. Forget blood, he was de only brudder me ever had.

I recalled the time when Misser Donaldson had just seasoned me. My scars were fresh, thick, and ugly. My defiant spirit was weakened.

I was so weary from my first week's labor that exhaustion had overwhelmed me in the cane field. Keverton did my work and his own on that blazing afternoon. He roused me when Misser Donaldson approached on his donkey.

"You save me," I had said to Keverton.

"Nuh worry youself," he responded. "Just gimme some of you chicken."

I cried again.

I'm not sure how long I stayed on that hilltop staring at the green leaves around me. I willed for death to harvest me so I could meet my ancestors.

Eventually, hunger nagged me. I struggled to my feet. The sun had just finished its day. I wanted to bless my eyes on Mama and liccle Hopie again. *Deat' can tek me after dat if it still want to.*

I headed south.

At times I had to hack away stiff shrubs, tangled bush, and stubborn stalks to clear a path. It was hard work because the blade of my billhook was blunt. The ache from my shoulder had now spread to my feet.

Many times I had to stop and sip my water. I could no longer see the dirt track so I tried to climb as high as possible. It was only the thought of seeing my family that kept me going. *Me nuh have by me side no blood brudder, sister, mama, or papa*, I recalled Keverton saying to me. *You de nearest ting me have to dat.*

I pushed on through my loss, my tears, the dense woodland, and my splitting feet.

Finally, I saw a light. It was far ahead and below me but the sight of it kept my foot and hope strong. As I descended, I could make out the dirt track once again. Fire torches lined its route. As I crept closer, I recognized the wheelhouse, our rendezvous point following the Frontier uprising. I whispered a quick prayer for Old Misser Cliff. White men down there were fixing fences. They were dressed just like the men we had fought in the battle. Two horses nibbled the grass beside them. I hoped they hadn't discovered where we had buried the mighty Cudgemon. *Me would hate it if dem disturb Cudgemon's final sleep.*

I waited in hope that they'd leave so I could cross the dirt path, check on Cudgemon's grave, and collect water from the stream. But once they had finished their work, they retired into the wheelhouse. I heard them singing strange songs. For a short moment I thought about stealing their horses. *Cyan you imagine dat, Keverton? Dem come outta de wheelhouse and cyan't find dem horse. You woulda laugh hard at dat. But then dem would know there was somebody out here so and dem would hunt me down. Dem would chop off me head and show me mama.*

Frustrated, I climbed again to higher terrain. I came upon footprints in the hills and followed them. This led me to Midgewood's place. The goats and chickens were gone but there was guava, mangoes, and June plums. They were spoiled but I didn't care. I ate greedily.

Fatigue caught me again and I slept until the sun was high. I was woken by the sound of trotting horses pulling carts. I sneaked down near to the dirt track and, spying through the bushes, watched white men giving out orders to slaves. Even young boys and girls helped mend white people cabins and fences. I couldn't see anybody working in the fields.

I hacked my way farther south, keeping to higher ground. I wondered if Midgewood ever watched Keverton and me at work.

Eventually, I had an elevated view of Misser Master's big house. *We shoulda burn it down. Why we never do dat?* For a short moment, I thought of Keverton's dream of the big house with the long staircase.

Many horses fed on the grass on the front lawn. Soldiers rested under long-branched trees. Slaves went about their miserable business. Smoke spiraled from the roof of the cookhouse. I sniffed ham and bacon. My stomach twisted and groaned with hunger. Older slaves tip-tapped with their tools, fixing doors and windows and erecting wooden posts. There wasn't any aroma of boiling cane in the air and I couldn't hear the crunching sound of cane rollers. For a short while, I wondered if I should try to see Papa. I quickly dismissed the idea. He'd only want me to be like him. *Tacky and de rest of de cane warriors all die for someting. Yes, mon. Me papa will die for dat damn cane roller when dem get it working again.*

I found the stream that trickled behind the pit toilet. Ignoring the stench, I washed my feet and re-freshed myself. I looked for a good spot that offered cover and laid low until dark.

20

THE OTHER SIDE OF THE MOUNTAIN

There were fire torches circling the big house. White men rode in and out on horses. The outside work of the slaves seemed to be done for the night, but I wasn't sure if my mama and her sisters were still toiling in the cookhouse.

I decided to make my way to her cabin. There were only three chickens in the coop near to the cabins. The hogpen was empty. The taste of meat tormented my tongue and I was almost tempted by the fattest chicken there. He lived for another day.

Something moved in the bush but it was only a bullfrog hopping about its business. Even that looked like a decent meal.

I crept to the window of Mama's cabin. For a few moments, I crouched below an open window.

I listened.

I heard two women whispering to each other. Someone else was snoring.

I tapped the frame of the window with my bill-hook. "Mama?"

The conversation stopped.

Silence. I only heard the cicadas and the infrequent gusts of wind passing through the trees. Sweat dampened my eyelashes.

"Mama?"

Should me stand up and present meself? No, Moa. Anybody could be inna de hut.

"Mama?"

Her head poked out of the window. She wore a stained white tie-head. Her eyes grew big and her mouth opened like she wanted to swallow the night. Her cheeks glistened under the stars. Suddenly, in a swift movement, she climbed through the window. She hugged me hard and stroked my head. "Me one son ah come back to me," she said. "Asase Ya listen to me! Me t'ought you were dead for true!"

"Nuh bother to stay here so," said a voice from within the cabin. It was Hamaya. "Me also pray to de Akan gods to spare you good foot!"

"Come, Mama," I said. "Let we step up to where de white mon nuh trod."

I grabbed her hand and led her beyond the pit

toilet. It was good to feel her hand in mine. Up we scrambled. Mama's clothes were just as stained as mine. We sat down behind the cover of thick bushes. Some small creature's eyes watched us from above. For a long while, she just gazed at me and cradled my face with her fingers. She caressed my cheeks and wiped the blood from my forehead. It was almost like she was checking that I wasn't a duppy or a spirit. "Me cyan't believe it," she said. "After we hear what happen to Tacky, we t'ought all de cane warriors dead."

"We ancestors will be mighty proud of him," I said. "Him meet dem in hot battle like de king he was. Somebody bawl out dat Tacky dead and gone but me never see him fall. Me never see too much of what happen. Nuff dust and confusion. Keverton pulled me away."

"Bless Keverton," she said. "Him always wanted to look after you."

Then she gave me a look. I knew what she was asking.

"Keverton dead, Mama."

She kept very still. Her gaze wouldn't leave me.

"Him . . ." I started again. "Him and de other surviving cane warriors have gone to de caves by de broad blue waters. Asase Ya, Nyame, and Bele Alua spirit inna de caves, Mama."

"So . . . so," Mama stuttered.

"So dem tek dem own life," I continued. "Dem promised to de gods dem will never be slave again. No back-ripper will stain dem backs no more. Dem will rise and tek dem stance again."

She dropped her head and I gently took her face into my palms.

"Keverton save me, Mama. Pray for him so him cyan reach we ancestors."

"Me will," she replied.

We shared our loss together. No words were needed.

"Ah whole heap of white mon ah come here so," Mama said after a while. She kept her voice low. "Dem say dem kill ever'body. Ah new master now living inna de big house—Misser Bannion, dem call him."

"Mama, what de white mon tell you about Tacky?"

Her head fell again.

"Mama?"

She took in a breath. "Misser Bannion call ah meeting 'pon de front lawn inna de afternoon," she said. "Him tell we dem kill Tacky and . . . cut off him head."

I knew he had fallen, but for a short moment my insides twisted and my heartbeat echoed inside my throat. I pleaded with my eyes for Mama to tell me this wasn't true. I already knew the answer.

She nodded and squeezed my hands. "Dem put

poor Tacky's head 'pon ah spike and put it on show in Spanish Town."

I couldn't speak. Tears fell freely. I prayed that his body would be buried beside a long tree and swift waters.

"Dem say dem killed ever'body," Mama repeated.

It took me a few minutes to take it all in.

"You cyan't stay here so, Moa. If dem find out you was part of de uprising, dem will kill you for true. Dem might even chop off you own head and put it 'pon show somewhere. You must tek up you good foot and go'way somewhere far."

"Me nuh know which way to go, Mama," I said.

"You tell me nuff times already how you wonder what's on de other side of de mountain."

I strained my eyes and peered into the east. I could just make out dark shapes beneath the stars.

"Me have to get you some food," Mama said.

A noise.

Rustling of leaves.

Scraping feet.

Both our heads snapped to the direction of the sounds. My muscles tensed. I raised my billhook.

Hamaya.

She pulled herself over the ridge and stood up. Her hands were covered in grit and soil. Mud painted her forehead. Her big eyes glared at me accusingly.

"Hamaya!" Mama called. "You follow we?"

"Of course," Hamaya said. "Me hear Moa's voice from de cabin. Me had to see him."

"*Wo ho te sen?*" I greeted her.

"*Me ho ye,*" Hamaya answered.

Mama didn't protest Hamaya's presence. She turned to me again. "There's ah piece of ham inna de cookhouse. Let me get dat for you and some vegetables. If you going to climb dat mighty hilltop you going to need it. Nuh let Hamaya talk off you ears. You cyan't stay here too long."

Mama slid down the slope. Hamaya stood with her hands on her hips and stared at me like I was an overseer.

"You lef' me," she said.

"Me never lef' you. Me went off to fight for you."

Hamaya shook her head. "Lef' me you lef' me!"

"Hamaya, try to understand."

"Me understand. Me nuh want to stay here so. No, mon."

Dem will soon come for me, I recalled Hamaya saying before the uprising. My belly crunched like the cane beneath Papa's rolling wheels.

I wasn't sure if I could be responsible for Hamaya's life. *Could me really look after her?*

"You nuh grow to you size yet," I said.

"Me foot strong," she said. "Me leg tough. Every

day me walk up to de millhouse wid me cart of cane. Me cyan climb any long mountaintop. And me cyan run fast like de north wind. Asase Ya know dat."

"Mama and liccle Hopie need somebody to look out for dem," I said.

"De older sisters cyan do dat. Moa, you cyan't leave me here so. Becah even before me grow to me size, white mon *will* tek me. Dem will tek me just like dem tek me mama. And me never see so much white mon here so."

I thought about it. Hamaya's face softened. Her eyes were full of hope as well as tears. Her long lashes were drenched. My heart felt her intense gaze. *Maybe she have de right to die for someting too if she have to. Or live for someting like meself.* I remembered what Keverton once said to me: *If you live for youself you live in vain, if you live for somebody else you live again.*

"You sure you foot strong?" I asked again.

"Maybe even stronger than your own good foot."

"Cyan you start ah fire?" I asked.

Hamaya smiled. "Me cyan start ah fire to burn de whole world. And dat fire cyan *never* be put out."

I nodded. "All right, all right . . . you cyan come wid me."

She ran up to me and flung her arms around my neck. "You always been ah big brudder for me," she said. "Me will never let you down. And anyway, inna de bush you need somebody to look after you."

I thought of Keverton. A sudden sadness filled me. I could almost smell him, see him, and listen to his words. I relived the echoed chants from the caves.

Moments later, I heard a voice.

Mama.

"Moa! Moa! Me nuh want to climb up again," she said. "Come down for you food. Me have ah piece of ham and some vegetables for you."

Hamaya descended the tricky slope with ridiculous ease. I followed her. Mama handed me a generous portion of salted ham that was wrapped in broad leaves. I hoped the white men wouldn't realize the food had gone missing. She gave vegetables to Hamaya and a small cooking pot.

"You . . . you know she want to come wid me?" I asked Mama.

Mama nodded. "Every night she say dat if you come back, she will go'long wid you."

"Me won't let you lef' me again," Hamaya said. "Come, we have to climb de big hill. And call out to me if you foot get tired."

"Tek some water before you go," Mama said. She went back into her cabin and returned with two wooden mugs. "Drink from de stream before you t'ink about climbing long hill," she said. "Find ah nice place for youself."

"And when me find dat nice place," I said, "me will come back for you. Yes, Mama. Me will come back for you when liccle Hopie foot get broad so she cyan walk good."

"She just about walking now," Mama said. "And when me rock her to sleep me tell her stories about her big brudder."

I smiled. "Me story nuh finish yet, Mama. When she understand, tell liccle Hopie dat me t'ink of her every night."

"Me will teach her de song me once sing to you. You remember it? *Nuh worry, children. Slavemaster have no god friend.*"

I nodded and grinned. "Me remember it, Mama."

"No matter what happen," said Mama, "Hopie will grow and know de story of Tacky, de mighty cane warrior, and her big brudder, Moa Umbassa. Yes, mon. Now tek up you good foot and go'long."

Hamaya and I hugged Mama together before we set off toward the shadowed hills in the east. I paused, turned around, and said, "De blood remembers."

"*Kwan so dwoodwoo,*" Mama called.

"Good travel," said Hamaya. "Dat's what you mama say."

"Me know, Hamaya," I replied.

"If me ever get bless wid any pickney," Hamaya added, "me will mek sure dem will remember too."

"And dem will back de evil against de wall," I said. "And stand firm and strong just like Tacky."

De blood will remember.

—THE END—

AUTHOR'S NOTE

My mother was raised in the small market town of Richmond in the St. Mary parish in northeast Jamaica. Richmond is adjacent to the Frontier and Trinity slave plantations where Tacky led his uprising in 1760. Pride flows through me in the still of the night when I consider the possibility of being a descendant of one of Tacky's mighty cane warriors. The blood certainly remembers.

My mother often relates tales of her childhood to me, the never-ending chores she did as a little girl and how excited she was when her father offered her reading material. Sometimes at night, she overheard her parents, family elders, and friends reminiscing about the distant past. The evils of slavery would arise in many hushed conversations. Various names would be repeated—Jamaican heroes Paul Bogle, Sam Sharpe, Queen Nanny of the Maroons, and indeed one elder mentioned that "de mighty Tacky once walked and worked dis very land before de 1760 Easter uprising. De blood remembers."

My father once took me on a day trip to visit the playwright Sir Noel Coward's holiday home, Firefly, near Port Maria. Little did I know at the time that the property and land was once owned by the notorious pirate and onetime governor of Jamaica, Sir Henry Morgan. Before the buccaneer first enjoyed the spectacular view of the ocean (1,200 feet above sea level), the real estate was a lookout post for the British military: Fort Haldane, where Tacky and his warriors fought and killed the soldiers stationed there. They seized their forty muskets and gunpowder there.

For a storyteller, I had no option. I was compelled to research Tacky's legend and the 1760 rebellion that occurred at Frontier, Trinity, and other plantations.

Backdropped by Burning Spear's "Jah a Guh Raid," Bob Marley and the Wailers' live version of "The Heathen," Eek-A-Mouse's "Do You Remember," and Gregory Isaacs's "Slave Master," I went to work.

I'm not embarrassed to admit that writing this narrative made me weep several times but also swelled my pride in the people who came before me and fought imperial savagery with immense bravery. Every single Jamaican should push out their chest when they hear Tacky's name mentioned. He and his fellow cane warriors are our glorious dead.

There is no doubt that the British Empire was one

of the most brutal and unforgiving in world history. They inflicted their own particular brand of holocaust. Between 1662 and 1807, Britain shipped over three million Africans across the Atlantic Ocean to British-owned colonies in the Caribbean. We can only hazard a guess at the thousands upon thousands who were murdered and perished through illness in transit.

The 1807 Slave Trade Act of the UK Parliament banned the slave trade in the British Empire, but slavery itself remained legal until the Slavery Abolition Act in 1833. In the same year, the UK government pledged £20 million in order to reimburse the owners of slaves—a huge sum even now but back in the mid-seventeenth century, an astronomical figure.

The slaves weren't paid a penny. Not even a farthing.

I'm reminded of Bob Marley's line in his classic song "Concrete Jungle": "*No chains around my feet but I'm not free.*"

It took the British taxpayer 182 years to pay it off. Indeed, descendants of slaves—like myself—have contributed to this blood debt.

It's for the above reason that I vigorously support claims for slavery reparations. Portia Simpson Miller, former prime minister of Jamaica, called for nonconfrontational discussions with the British government about reparations in 2013. The Jamaican minister of culture, gender, entertainment, and sport, Olivia

"Babsy" Grange, said, "In the same way we take action in this House [of Representatives] to clear the names of our national heroes and freedom fighters, we must also take action to ensure that reparations are paid for all that our ancestors endured under the evil system of slavery, having been brought to this island in chains and branded like animals . . . We must pursue reparations. The great wrong must be set right . . ."

Lastly, I want to mention two academic texts that helped inspire me to write *Cane Warriors: The Black Jacobins* by the great Trinidadian writer C.L.R. James; and *Inglorious Empire* by Shashi Tharoor.